D0066131

The Case of the Calendar Girl

Erle Stanley Gardner

Thorndike Press • Thorndike, Maine

Library of Congress Cataloging in Publication Data:

Gardner, Erle Stanley, 1889-1970.
   The case of the calendar girl / Erle Stanley Gardner.
      p.   cm.
   ISBN 1-56054-388-4 (alk. paper : lg. print)
   1. Large type books.   I. Title.
[PS3513.A6322C34   1992]   92-8694
813'.52—dc20   CIP

Thorndike Large Print® All Time Favorites Series edition
published in 1992 by arrangement with William Morrow
& Company, Inc.

Cover design by Ron Walotsky.

The tree indicium is a trademark of Thorndike Press.

This book is printed on acid-free, high opacity paper. ∞

Foreword

I consider my friend, Dr. Hubert Winston Smith, one of the outstanding figures in the field of legal medicine, just as I consider legal medicine far more important than it is generally considered in the public mind.

Dr. Hubert Winston Smith is not only a doctor of medicine but an attorney at law as well. He is, moreover, a trial attorney of unusual ability.

Some years ago he was appointed special counsel to represent a veteran of World War II who had been convicted of homicide on circumstantial evidence and sentenced to the electric chair. Dr. Smith was able to bring out a mass of new evidence and present this evidence so convincingly that the conviction was reversed by the Louisiana Supreme Court.

Not only is Dr. Smith a professor of law, a teacher of evidence and of legal medicine at the Law School of the University of Texas, but he is also Professor of Legal Medicine in the Medical School of that University, and is

Director of the Law Science Institute. In fact, it would take more space than is presently available simply to list Dr. Smith's honors and academic distinctions.

It is under his guidance that legal medicine classes for doctors and trial lawyers are being held throughout the country. In these classes, members of both the medical and legal professions are given an opportunity to study the highly technical field of medical evidence as applied to law.

But what interests me most of all about Dr. Smith is his philosophical outlook on life. This trained scientist feels that the time has come when man should concentrate on what Dr. Smith refers to as "psychic income" rather than income on a dollars-and-cents basis.

Recently I had occasion to visit a young man who was confined in jail on a charge that was almost certain to result in a prison sentence. This young man was making a goodfaith effort to analyze the reasons which had caused him to become a criminal. At length, he said, "I wish that while I was getting my education someone had pointed out to me a little more clearly the basic difference between right and wrong."

This was a simple statement, yet when we analyze it, it has far-reaching repercussions. It was a statement that came from a young man whose life had been blasted because he hadn't stopped to think of the basic difference between right and wrong.

Dr. Hubert Winston Smith is a man at the other end of the human spectrum. He is as highly educated as any man can expect to be. He is a master of all branches of medicine including that of psychiatry. He is a shrewd, ingenious, well-trained, capable trial attorney. He is one of the outstanding educators in the field of legal medicine, and his life is devoted to increasing the field of human knowledge.

And Dr. Smith feels that it is time for us as a nation to pay more attention to "psychic income."

So I dedicate this book to my friend:

HUBERT WINSTON SMITH, A.B., M.B.A., LL.B., M.D.

ERLE STANLEY GARDNER

Cast of Characters

Chapter 1

George Ansley slowed his car, looking for Meridith Borden's driveway.

A cold, steady drizzle soaked up the illumination from his headlights. The windshield wipers beat a mechanical protest against the moisture which clung to the windshield with oily tenacity. The warm interior of the car caused a fogging of the glass, which Ansley wiped off from time to time with his handkerchief.

Meridith Borden's estate was separated from the highway by a high brick wall, surmounted with jagged fragments of broken glass embedded in cement.

Abruptly the wall flared inward in a sweeping curve, and the gravel driveway showed white in Ansley's headlights. The heavy iron gates were open. Ansley swung the wheel and followed the curving driveway for perhaps a quarter of a mile until he came to the stately, old-fashioned mansion, relic of an age of solid respectability.

For a moment Ansley sat in the automobile after he had shut off the motor and the headlights. It was hard to bring himself to do what he had to do, but try as he might, he could think of no other alternative.

He left the car, climbed the stone steps to the porch and pressed a button which jangled musical chimes in the deep interior of the house.

A moment later the porch was suffused with brilliance, and Ansley felt he was undergoing thorough, careful scrutiny. Then the door was opened by Meridith Borden himself.

"Ansley?" Borden asked.

"That's right," Ansley said, shaking hands. "I'm sorry to disturb you at night. I wouldn't have telephoned unless it had been a matter of considerable importance — at least to me."

"That's all right, quite all right," Borden said. "Come on in. I'm here alone this evening. Servants all off. . . . Come on in. Tell me what's the trouble."

Ansley followed Borden into a room which had been fixed up into a combination den and office. Borden indicated a comfortable chair, crossed over to a portable bar, said, "How about a drink?"

"I could use one," Ansley admitted. "Scotch and soda, please."

Borden filled glasses. He handed one to Ansley, clinked the ice in his drink, and stood by the bar, looking down at Ansley from a position of advantage.

He was tall, thick-chested, alert, virile and arrogant. There was a contemptuous attitude underlying the veneer of rough and ready cordiality which he assumed. It showed in his eyes, in his face and, at times, in his manner.

Ansley said, "I'm going broke."

"Too bad," Borden commented, without the slightest trace of sympathy. "How come?"

"I have the contract on this new school job out on 94th Street," Ansley said.

"Bid too cheap?" Borden inquired.

"My bid was all right."

"Labor troubles?"

"No. Inspector troubles."

"How come?"

"They're riding me all the time. They're making me tear out and replace work as fast as I put it in."

"What's the matter? Aren't you following specifications?"

"Of course I'm following specifications, but it isn't a question of specifications. It's a question of underlying hostility, of pouncing on every little technicality to make me do work over, to hamper me, to hold up the job, to delay the work."

Borden made clucking noises of sympathy.

His eyes, hard and appraising, remained fixed on Ansley.

"I protested to the inspector," Ansley said. "He told me, 'Why don't you get smart and see Meridith Borden?'"

"I don't think I like that," Borden said.

Ansley paid no attention to the comment. "A friend of mine told me, 'You damn fool. Go see Borden.' And . . . well, here I am."

"What do you want me to do?"

"Call off your dogs."

"They're not *my* dogs."

"I didn't mean it that way."

"You said it that way."

There was a moment of silence.

"How much are you going to make on the job?" Borden asked.

"If they'll let me alone and let me follow specifications according to any reasonable interpretation, I'll have a fifty-thousand-dollar profit."

"Too bad you're having trouble," Borden said. "I'd want a set of the specifications and a statement by you as to the type of trouble you've been having. If I decide you are being unjustly treated, I'll threaten a full-scale investigation. I don't think you'll have any more trouble. I'd need money, of course."

"Of course," Ansley said dryly.

"And," Borden went on, "after we start

16

working together you won't have *any* trouble with the inspectors. Just make your stuff so it's good construction, so that it'll stand up, and that's all you need to worry about. Don't measure the placement of your structural steel with too much accuracy. Make your mix contain just enough concrete to do the job, and don't worry about having absolutely uniform percentages."

"That isn't what I wanted," Ansley said. "I only wanted to have a reasonable break."

"You'll get it," Borden promised. "Mail me a retainer of two thousand dollars tomorrow, pay five thousand from the next two progress payments you get, and give me five per cent of the final payment. Then we'll talk things over on the next job. I understand you're planning to bid on the overhead crossing on Telephone Avenue?"

"I've thought about it. I'd like to get cleaned up on this job and get my money out of it first."

"Okay. See me about that overhead crossing before you put in your bid. We'll talk it over. I can help you. A good public relations man who knows the ropes can do a lot on jobs of this kind."

"I'm satisfied he can," Ansley said bitterly.

"I wish you'd seen me before you took that school job," Borden went on. "There might have been more in it for both of us. You didn't have any public relations expert to represent your interest in connection with the bidding?"

"No. Why should I need a public relations expert just to submit a bid?"

Borden shrugged his shoulders. The gesture was eloquent.

Ansley finished his drink. "I'm sorry that I had to bother you at this hour of the night, but the inspector found two places in the wall where he claimed the steel was incorrectly spaced. It didn't amount to more than a quarter of an inch, but he demanded I conform to specifications. I can't tear out the whole wall, and to try to cut and patch now would be prohibitive."

Borden said, "See that inspector tomorrow and tell him to take another measurement. I think the steel's all right. The rods may have been bent a little off center. Quit worrying about it. Tomorrow's a new day."

Ansley put down the drink, got up, hesitated, then said, "Well, I guess I'll be getting on."

"I'm glad you dropped in, Ansley," Borden said, "and I'll take care of you to the best of my ability. I feel quite certain you won't have any more trouble with the inspectors. They don't like adverse publicity any better than anyone else, and, after all, I'm a public relations expert."

Borden laughed and moved to accompany Ansley to the door.

"I can find my way out all right," Ansley said.

"No, no, I'll see you to the door. I'm all alone here tonight. Sorry."

He escorted Ansley to the door, said good night, and Ansley went down the steps into the cold rain.

He knew that his trouble with the inspectors was over, but he knew that the trouble with his self-respect had just begun.

They had told him at the start that it was foolish to try to build anything without getting in touch with Meridith Borden. Ansley had thought he could get by, by being scrupulously fair and conforming to the specifications. He was rapidly finding out how small a part fairness and specifications played in the kind of job he was getting into now.

Ansley sent his car crunching along the gravel driveway. His anger at himself and the conditions which had forced him to go to Meridith Borden made him resentful. He knew that he was driving too fast, knew that it wasn't going to do him any good to try to hurry away from Meridith Borden's palatial estate on the outskirts of the city, knew that it wasn't going to do him any good to try to get away from himself. He had lost something important in that interview; a part of him that he couldn't afford to lose, but he had yielded to the inexorable pressure of economic necessity.

Ansley swung the wheel around the last curve in the driveway and slowed for the main highway as he saw the iron gates.

It was at that moment that he saw the headlights on the road swinging toward him.

Apparently the driver of the oncoming car intended to turn in at the gate, and was cutting the corner before realizing a car was coming. The smooth, black surface of the road was slippery with an oily coating from the first rain in weeks.

For a brief moment headlights blazed into Ansley's windshield, then the other car swirled through the gate into a sickening, skidding turn. The rear fender of the car brushed against the bumper of Ansley's car.

In vain Ansley tried to bring his car to a stop. He felt the jar of impact, saw the careening car tilt upward, swerve from the driveway. He heard a crash, dimly saw the hedge sway under the impact, heard another jarring sound and then silence.

Ansley braked his car to a stop just outside the gates. Without bothering to shut off the motor or dim the headlights, he scrambled out from behind the wheel, leaving the front left-hand door swinging wide open. He ran back through the soggy gravel to the gap in the hedge.

He could see the other car only as a dim, dark bulk. The motor was no longer running, the lights were off. He had the impression that the car was lying over on its side, but he couldn't be certain. The machine had crashed through the hedge, but there remained enough broken twigs and jagged branches to make progress extremely difficult and hazardous.

"Is everyone all right?" Ansley asked, standing midway through the tangle of the jagged hedge.

There was no answer, only a dead silence.

Ansley's eyes were gradually becoming more accustomed to the darkness. He plunged forward, pushing his way through the water-soaked leaves.

A projecting snag caught the leg of Ansley's trousers, tripped him, threw him forward. He heard ripping cloth, felt a sharp pain along his shin. Then, as he threw out his hands to protect himself, his right hand was snagged by the sharp projection of a broken branch. The ground was sloping sharply, and Ansley found himself with his head lower than his feet. It was with difficulty that he got to his knees, and then once more to a standing position.

The car was directly in front of him now, only some twenty feet away. By this time he could see plainly that the car was resting on the right-hand side of the top.

"Hello," Ansley called. "Is everybody all right?"

Again there was no answer.

"Is anybody hurt?" Ansley asked.

The night silence was broken only by the gurgling noises of liquids draining from the car. There was the harsh odor of raw gasoline.

Ansley knew he didn't dare to strike a match. He remembered then, belatedly, that he kept a small flashlight in the glove compartment of his car. He ran back, floundering through the hedge, opened the glove compartment of his car and returned with the flashlight.

This light, carried for emergencies, had been in the glove compartment for a long time. The battery was all but dead. The bulb furnished a fitful reddish glow which Ansley knew wouldn't last long. In order to save the battery, he switched out the light and again floundered through the broken hedge in the dark. He approached the car, saw that one of the doors was swinging partially open. He thrust his arm inside the car and turned on the flashlight.

There was no one inside.

Ansley moved around the front of the car, holding the flashlight in front of him. What should have been a beam of bright light was now only a small cone of faint illumination. It was, however, sufficient to show the girl's feet and ankles, feet which were eloquently motionless.

Ansley hurried around so that he could see the rest of the form which lay huddled there on the wet grass.

She had evidently been thrown to the ground and had skidded forward. The legs were smooth, shapely and well rounded. The momentum of the young woman's slide had left her legs exposed to the thighs, her skirts rumpled into a twisted ball. Ansley raised the flashlight, saw one arm twisted up and over the face, and then the light failed completely.

Instinctively, and without thinking, Ansley threw the useless flashlight from him, bent over the young woman's body and in the darkness groped for her wrist.

He found a pulse, a faint but regular heartbeat.

Ansley straightened and started groping his way across to the gravel driveway, only to find that the hedge barred his progress. He moved along parallel with the hedge, raised his voice and shouted, "Help!" at the top of his lungs.

The soggy darkness swallowed up the cry, and Ansley, annoyed at the thick hedge which kept him from the open gravel driveway, lowered his shoulder and prepared to crash through the intertwined branches.

It was then he heard the faint, moaning call from behind him.

Ansley paused and listened. This time he heard a tremulous cry of "Help! Help!"

Once more Ansley turned and groped his way back through the darkness to the overturned car.

The young woman was sitting up now, a vague figure in the darkness. Ansley could see the blurred white oval of her face, her two hands and the lighter outline of flesh above her stockings.

"Are you hurt?" Ansley asked.

By way of answer she instinctively pulled down her skirt.

"Where am I?" she asked.

"I don't know."

"Let's find out," Ansley said, dropping down beside her. "Any broken bones?"

"Who . . . who are you?"

"I was driving the car that you . . . ran into."

"Oh."

"Tell me, are you all right? Try moving

your arms, your legs."

"I've moved my arms," she said. "My . . . my legs . . . Yes, I'm all right. Help me up, will you, please?"

She extended a hand and Ansley took it. After two abortive attempts, she managed to get to her feet. She stood, wobbling for a moment, then swayed against him.

Ansley supported her with an arm around her waist, a hand under her armpit on the other side. "Take it easy," he said.

"Where . . where am I?"

"You were just turning in at the driveway of the Meridith Borden estate when you apparently lost control of your car," Ansley said, choosing his words carefully, not wishing to accuse the shaken young woman of having hit him, but carefully avoiding any admission that his car had hit hers.

"Oh, yes," she said, "I remember now. . . . There was something in the road ahead, a dead cat or something. I didn't know what it was. I swerved the car slightly and then all of a sudden I was dizzy, going around and around. I saw headlights and then there was a crash. I felt myself going over, and the next thing I knew, I was sitting here in the grass. I'm . . . I'm all right now. My head is clearing rapidly."

"Were you alone?" Ansley asked.

"Yes."

"Do you have anything in the car?"

"Nothing except my purse. I'll get that. Do you have a flashlight?"

"No. I had one that was just about completely run-down. I was able to get a few minutes' light from the thing before the battery ran down completely."

"Do you have a match?"

"Don't strike a match," Ansley warned. "There's gasoline draining out of the motor somewhere, or out of the gas tank."

"I can find it," she said. "At least I hope I can."

"Can I get it for you? Can I — ?"

"No," she said, "I'll get it."

She stooped, crawled through the open door, and once more Ansley saw the rounded flesh above her stocking tops as she struggled back, getting out through the door feet first.

"Get it?" Ansley asked.

"I got it," she said. "Heavens! I'll bet I was a spectacle *that* time."

Ansley said, "It's dark. Thank heavens you're not hurt. The first thing for us to do is to get you where you want to go, and then we'll send a tow car out and notify Borden."

"I'll take care of that," she said hastily. "Don't bother about it. And don't worry about the accident. It wasn't your fault. I think it was just one of those unavoidable things.

26

Your car isn't damaged, is it?"

"I didn't look," Ansley said, "but I don't think so. The way it felt you just grazed my bumper."

"Let's go take a look," she said.

"Do you have anything in there besides your purse?"

"That's all. There's a raincoat in there somewhere, but that can wait until the tow car shows up."

"Can I get it for you?"

"No, I know about where it is."

"It's dark," Ansley said.

She said, "Yes, but I think I can find it."

She wiggled her way into the car again, came out pulling a coat after her and said, "Okay, let's go."

"Now, we're supposed to do something about this, I think," Ansley said, as he led the way through the hedge. "I think we're supposed to make a report or something."

"Oh, sure, we're supposed to check one another's driving licenses and all that. We'll have time to talk that over while you're driving me into town. You *are* headed toward the city, aren't you?"

"Yes."

"Well, that's fine."

"I'll take you anywhere you want to go," Ansley said.

"Do you know the Ancordia Apartments?"

"No, I'm not familiar with them."

"Well, turn off — I'll show you. Just go on in on the freeway."

"All right," Ansley said. "I'll take a look at my car, but I'm quite certain there's no damage done."

Ansley looked at his car, found a dented fender and a scrape of paint on the bumper.

"No damage to my car," he said.

"Do I just hop in?" she asked.

Ansley laughed and held the door open. "Hop in," he invited.

Ansley had a chance to size the young woman up as the light in the interior of the car disclosed reddish hair, even, regular features, dark brownish eyes, a firm chin and a good figure.

"We may as well get acquainted," she said, laughing. "I'm Beatrice Cornell. I live in the Ancordia Apartments. My friends call me Bee for short."

"George Ansley," he told her. "A struggling contractor trying to get by."

"And," she observed, taking out a note-book, "I suppose, in order to comply with the amenities of the situation, I've got to have the license number of your automobile."

"JYJ 113," he told her.

"Mine is CVX 266. I'm all covered by in-

28

surance and I suppose you are."

He nodded.

"Then we can forget the legal aspects of the situation and discuss the personal. Can you tell me exactly what happened?"

"Not very well," he said. "I was just coming out of the driveway. You were coming along the road, and I thought you were turning in at the driveway."

She shook her head. "I was trying to avoid this thing in the road, a clod of earth, a dead cat or something. The car swung out all right around the obstruction, whatever it was, and then when I started to straighten, I couldn't. I saw your headlights right ahead of me. Then they pinwheeled off to one side, then I was rolling over, and that's the last I remember. . . . Can you go on from there?"

"I got out of my car and ran through the hedge to see if there had been any damage," Ansley said, "and you were out like a light. Evidently you'd hit the ground feet first and skidded along on the damp grass."

"You had a flashlight?"

"I had a worn-out flashlight. The batteries didn't last long."

She glanced at him archly. "And a good thing, too — from my point of view," she said.

"Unfortunately, I couldn't see much," he told her.

She laughed. "Oh, well, legs are standard equipment anyway, and thanks to the wet grass, I didn't lose any skin although I feel a little muddy in places."

Ansley took out his wallet, handed it to her, and said, "My driving license is in the cellophane compartment there. Copy the number and the address."

"Oh, that isn't at all necessary," she said. "After all, that's a formality reserved for strangers who intend to sue each other. I hope we'll be friends."

"Believe me," Ansley said, "I can't tell you how relieved I am that you're not hurt."

"I'm all right. No doubt I'll be a little sore tomorrow."

"You're sure that's all it is?"

"Sure."

"You must have had something of a concussion," Ansley said. "You certainly were out cold."

"Probably hit the back of my head on the ground," she said, "but it's been hit before. I've done some skiing and swimming and what with one thing and another I've had my share of knocks."

"Rather an active career," Ansley said.

She laughed. "I'm an active woman. I like

30

action. . . . You said the property belonged to Meridith Borden?"

"Yes."

"He's a politician, isn't he?"

"Public relations is the way he describes himself."

"That's just another way of saying lobbyist, isn't it? I've read comments about him. Some people seem to think he's a man with a cloven hoof."

"I guess any person in politics has his share of enemies," Ansley said noncommittally.

"Do you know him?"

"I've met him."

"You were coming from there?"

"That's right."

"Oh, all right," she said, laughing. "I didn't want to pry into your private affairs. I was just making conversation."

"I didn't mean to be secretive," he said.

"Perhaps you didn't mean to be, but you are. I think you're naturally secretive. Do you know, George, I'm getting just a little headache. If you don't mind, I'm going to settle back and close my eyes."

"Now, look here," Ansley said, "you're going to a doctor. You've had a concussion, and —"

"Don't be silly!" she protested. "I don't need a doctor. If I do, there's a doctor who lives in the same apartment house. I'll get him to give me a sedative. Now, don't be a silly boy, just go ahead and drive me to the Ancordia and forget it.

"You turn on Lincoln Avenue and go to 81st Street, and then turn right and —"

"Oh, I know where it is now," Ansley said. "I'll take you there."

She settled back against the cushions, closed her eyes.

After some five minutes Ansley eased the car to a stop in front of the Ancordia Apartments.

His passenger opened her eyes, seemed dazed for a moment, sighed sleepily, leaned over against him. Her chin came up as her head cradled against the side of his arm. Her lips were half-parted, her eyes were dreamy as she raised and lowered the lids.

"Well, here we are," Ansley said.

"Here — Who . . . ?"

"Look here," Ansley said, bending over to look into her face, "are you quite all right?"

Her eyes opened then. For a moment they were fastened on his with a provocative smile. Her lips remained parted. Her chin tilted just a little more.

Ansley bent forward and kissed her.

She sighed tremulously; her warm lips clung to his, then suddenly, as though wakening from a dream, she stiffened, pushed him back and, for a moment, seemed indignant.

"I was asleep," she said. "I —"

"I'm sorry," Ansley said.

Abruptly she laughed. "Don't be. I guess I led with my chin. . . . I was half-asleep thinking of one of my boy friends."

"I couldn't resist the temptation," Ansley said contritely. "I —"

"Don't apologize. Men aren't supposed to resist temptation. That's in the feminine department. Am I going to see you again?"

"I'll take you to your apartment," Ansley said.

"Indeed you won't," she told him. "I'm quite all right."

"No, no, I want to see you up."

"Well, as far as the street door," she compromised. "After all, you're going to have to leave your car double-parked."

Ansley hurried around the car to help her out, but she had the door open before he arrived. She gave him her hand, slid out from the seat, paused, said, "I'll bet I'm mud from head to toe."

She moved her skirt up along the nylon stocking with a gesture that seemed entirely natural and uninhibited, then suddenly laughed, let her skirt drop, and said, "I guess I'd better make that inspection in the privacy of my apartment."

She ran lightly up the steps to the apartment, fumbled in her purse, said, "Oh, dear, I left my key at the office again. I'll have to get one of my friends to let me in."

She pushed on the button and a moment later a buzzer announced the latch was being released on the street door.

She opened the door for an inch or two, held it open with her foot, turned to Ansley and said, "I'm going to let you kiss me again, George. Either my dreams deceived me or you're an expert. I'm fully awake now."

Ansley swept her into his arms.

His kiss was long. Her response was practiced.

"I'm fully awake now, myself," Ansley said, looking at her hungrily.

She smiled at him. "Mustn't try to make too much progress the first night, George. I hope I see you again. Give me a ring. Bye now."

She slipped through the door.

Ansley stood for a moment watching the slowly closing door, hearing the click of the latch as the door closed.

He turned, retraced his steps to his automobile and sat for a moment behind the wheel, his forehead puckered in thought.

Chapter 2

Perry Mason and Della Street, enjoying a leisurely dinner, had sat through the floor show, had danced twice and were finishing up on brandy and Benedictine when Della Street looked up with a slight frown of annoyance at the young man who was approaching their table with a businesslike directness which indicated he had some definite objective in mind.

"Mr. Mason," the man said, "my name is George Ansley. I was finishing a cocktail here earlier this evening just as you came in. I know you by sight. I dislike to intrude in this way, but . . . well, I'm in need of some legal advice. It's a minor matter, something you can tell me offhand. Here's my card. If you'll just answer a question and then send me a bill, I'll . . . well, I'll certainly appreciate the favor."

Mason said, "I'm sorry, but I'm —" Suddenly, at the look in Ansley's eyes, he changed his mind. "Sit down, have a drink and tell us about it. This is Miss Street, my confidential secretary. For your information, Ansley, I do mostly trial work and I only take the cases that interest me. Somehow or other that has led me to gravitate toward the defense of persons accused of murder, and, unless you want to go out and commit a murder, I'm afraid you're not going to interest me."

"I know, I know," Ansley said. "This is just a minor matter, but it may be important to me."

"Well, what is it?" Mason asked.

"I was driving my car. I left here to keep a business appointment. The roads were wet, and a car driven by a young woman skidded into me and overturned."

"Much damage?" Mason asked.

"Virtually no damage to my car, but the other car was, I'm afraid, pretty completely wrecked. The car was in a skid when it hit me, and it went off the road, through a hedge and rolled over."

"Anybody hurt?"

"No, and — That's what bothers me."

"Go ahead," Mason said.

"A young woman was driving the car. She seems to be a delightful personality and she . . . well, I guess she liked me and somehow I — To tell you the truth, I don't know how I feel about her, Mr. Mason. When I was with her I felt that I liked her, and she certainly was attractive."

"Go on," Mason said.

"After I left, I began to realize that there was something terribly peculiar about the whole episode. She sort of led me along and . . . I kissed her a couple of times and I didn't think of too much else. I . . . well, here's the point, Mr. Mason. She was unconscious for a while, and then she came to. She seems to be feeling quite all right, but I've heard a lot about these cases of concussion. I suppose I should notify my insurance company. I'll take care of that all right, but what about the police? That's the thing that bothers me. Should I report the accident to the police?"

"The young woman was unconscious?" Mason said.

"That's right."

"And the car was damaged?"

"Yes."

"What kind was it?"

"It was a good-looking Cadillac, a late model."

"Get the license number?"

"Yes. It was CVX 266."

"Notify the police," Mason said. "Where did the accident happen?"

"That's just it, Mr. Mason. I . . . I don't want to notify the police unless I absolutely must."

"Why?" Mason asked.

"Well," Ansley said, "that's something of

a story and — Look here, Mr. Mason, I know you're a busy man, I know you work under quite a strain, I know you're trying to relax here tonight, and I feel like a heel, but the man who handles my legal business is out of town at the moment and I don't know anyone else. I saw you here and . . . well, this may be very, very important to me. I need the best in the line of legal advice."

"Why is it important?" Mason asked. "And why don't you want to report it to the Highway Patrol?"

"Because I'm a contractor. I'm contracting on some city jobs and they've put the bite on me."

"Who has?"

Ansley shrugged his shoulders and said, "How do I know? All I know is that the inspectors are making life impossible for me. I've been told to tear out a whole section of wall because a couple of pieces of structural steel were less than an inch out of place. I have inspectors hanging around the job looking things over with a microscope. . . . Well, I knew the answer. I put off doing what had to be done as long as I could, but now it's a question of whether I make a profit on the job or whether the thing wipes me out. This is one of my first big jobs. I've stretched my credit to the limit, and everything I have is riding along on that job."

"I still don't get what you're trying to tell me," Mason said.

"I was given the tip that the remedy for my troubles was to see Meridith Borden. I went out and saw him. The accident occurred just as I was leaving his grounds. The other car has rolled over and is on his grounds. I don't want to make a report to the Highway Patrol which will show I was leaving Meridith Borden's house. If it should get written up in the newspaper and — Well, you can see the position I'm in."

"Forget it," Mason said, "but notify your insurance carrier. And, of course, you've got to take a chance that the girl wasn't hurt. She seemed all right?"

"She seemed all right," Ansley said, "and yet there's something that isn't all right."

Mason glanced across at Della Street's disapproving face. "Now you've got me interested," he said. "Tell me about it. Do you know the girl's name?"

"Oh, yes, of course. I got her name."

"What is it?"

"Beatrice Cornell. She lives at the Ancordia Apartments."

"See her driving license?" Mason asked.

"No."

"Why not?"

"Well, that's one of the things that I got to thinking about later. She acted so peculiarly about the entire accident. The — Well, it was a funny thing, but I know she lied about one thing. She was deliberately turning her car into the driveway to Borden's house when she lost control of it, and it went into a skid. But she tried to tell me she didn't know Borden and was simply driving along the highway when she swerved to avoid a cat or something on the road, and —"

"Tell me about it," Mason said. "Start at the beginning and tell me the whole thing."

Della Street sighed, produced a shorthand notebook from her purse, pushed the half-emptied glass of brandy and Benedictine to one side and started taking notes.

Ansley told the entire story.

Mason's forehead creased in a frown. "You say this girl was unconscious?"

"Yes. There was a steady pulse, but it was thin and weak."

"Then you started for the house and she screamed and you ran back?"

"Yes."

"And the minute you ran back she seemed to be in full possession of her faculties?"

"Yes."

"You saw this young woman lying there unconscious with her legs and thighs exposed.

40

Your flashlight was working then?"

"Yes."

"What did she look like?"

"Well, of course, I had only a very general impression while she was lying there on the ground. Later on in the car I had a chance to see more of her.

"She was nice-looking, rather young — oh, say twenty-four or five and her hair was sort of a reddish brown. I think her eyes were dark brown. She had even, regular teeth which flashed when she smiled, and she seemed to smile easily."

"Now," Mason said, "let's concentrate on her shoes. Can you remember anything about her shoes?"

"Her shoes? Why?"

"I'm just asking," Mason said.

"Why, yes, they were sort of a brown. They were sort of dark with open toes."

Mason said, "All right. *She* told *you* she didn't want a doctor. *I'm* going to let her tell *me*. I'm going to ring her up and tell her I'm your attorney, that I want to send a doctor around to look at her and make certain she's all right."

"She'll refuse," Ansley said.

"Then we'll have made the offer," Mason told him. "Up to this time, it's your word against hers. Now *I'll* call up as your attorney, and she'll refuse to see a doctor and that will be that."

Mason nodded to Della Street. "Look up Beatrice Cornell, Della. See if she has a phone listed. If she doesn't, we'll have to get her through the Ancordia Apartments."

Della Street nodded, pushed back her chair and went to the telephone booth.

A moment later she beckoned Perry Mason, and, when the lawyer crossed over to the booth, Della said, "May I speak with Miss Beatrice Cornell, please? Yes . . . This is Miss Street. I'm the secretary for Mr. Mason, the attorney. He wants to talk with you. . . . Yes, Perry Mason. . . . No, I'm not fooling. Will you hold the line a moment, please . . . ? Yes. . . . My name is Street. S-t-r-e-e-t. I'm speaking for Mr. Mason. He's right here. Will you hold the line, please?"

Mason stepped into the booth.

"Miss Cornell?" he asked into the telephone.

"Yes."

"I'm Perry Mason, the lawyer."

"Say, just what sort of a gag *is* this?" the voice on the line demanded. "I thought I'd heard them all, but this is a new one."

"And why does it have to be a gag?" Mason asked.

The voice over the telephone was pleasing

to the ear, but an element of humorous skepticism was quite apparent. "My friends," she said, "know of my admiration for Mr. Mason. I make no secret of it and I suppose this is someone's idea of a gag. But go right ahead. I'll ride along with it. Let's suppose that you're Perry Mason, the attorney, and I'm the Queen of Sheba. Where do we go from here?"

"As it happens," Mason said, "I'm calling you on behalf of a client."

The voice suddenly lost its humorous skepticism and took on a note of genuine curiosity.

"The name of the client?"

"George Ansley," Mason said. "Does the name mean anything to you?"

"Should it?"

"Yes."

"It doesn't."

"He is the one who took you home a short time ago."

"Took me home?"

"From the automobile accident."

"What automobile accident are you talking about, Mr. Mason?"

"The accident in which your car was overturned. You have a Cadillac, I believe, the license CVX 266?"

She laughed. "I am a working girl, Mr. Mason. I haven't had a car for several years. All I have is an interest or an equity or whatever you want to call it in the public buses. I have been here in my apartment all evening, reading, as it happens, a mystery story, and hardly anticipating that I was going to be called in connection with one."

"And you live at the Ancordia Apartments?"

"That's right."

"Miss Cornell, this may be a matter of some importance. Would you mind giving me a physical description of yourself?"

"Why should I?" she asked.

"Because, as I told you, it may be a matter of some importance. I think perhaps someone has been using your name."

She hesitated a moment, then said, "I'll give you the description that appears on my driving license, acting on the assumption that perhaps this *is* Perry Mason. I am thirty-three years of age, I am a brunette, my eyes are dark, I am five feet, four inches in height, I weigh 122 pounds, and I'm trying to take off five of those pounds. Now, is there anything else I can tell you?"

"Thank you," Mason said, "you have been of the greatest help. I am afraid someone has been using your name. Do you know anyone who might have used your name?"

"No."

"Someone perhaps who lives in the same

apartment house?"

"I know of no one, Mr. Mason. . . . Tell me, is this on the level? Is this really on the up-and-up?"

"It is," Mason said. "A young woman was in an automobile accident earlier this evening. Mr. Ansley offered to drive her home. She gave him the name of Beatrice Cornell, the address of the Ancordia Apartments. This man drove her to that address. She thanked him and went in."

"Can you describe her?"

Mason, suddenly cautious, said, "I haven't as yet checked on her physical description with my client, but I might be able to call you back later on. Say perhaps tomorrow sometime."

"I wish you would," she said. "I'm very curious, and if this is really *the* Perry Mason with whom I'm talking, please accept my apologies for my initial skepticism. May I say that this was due to the fact that all my friends know I am a fan of yours. I have followed your legal adventures with considerable interest and enjoy reading about your cases in the newspapers."

"Thanks a lot," Mason told her. "I'm honored."

"*I'm* the one that's honored," she said.

"You'll probably hear from me later," Mason told her. "Good night."

Mason hung up the phone, frowned at Della Street, said, "Ring up Paul Drake at the Drake Detective Agency, Della. Ask him to get busy at once on a car having the license plates of CVX 266. I want to find out about it fast. I'll go back and rejoin Ansley."

"Well?" Ansley asked as Mason returned to the table.

Mason smiled. "She says she wasn't in any automobile accident, that she's been home all evening, that she doesn't know what it's all about. The description, according to her driving license, is age, thirty-three, brunette, dark eyes, height, five-feet-four, weight, 122 pounds."

Ansley frowned. "I don't think the woman in the car could have been more than thirty. I'd say maybe twenty-eight. That weight is a little heavy, and I'm quite certain the hair was reddish brown. I . . . . well, I just don't know."

"What about the height?"

"That's another thing. I think she was more than five feet, four inches. Of course, I don't remember all the details. She jumped in the car and then I —"

"But she was standing alongside of you," Mason said. "What happened when you said good night?"

"I kissed her."

"All right," Mason said, "get a visual recall of that event. How was she when you kissed her? Did she tilt her chin up, or was her face more nearly on a level with yours? How tall are you?"

"Five-feet-eleven."

"All right. Did you bend over when you kissed her?"

"Slightly."

"You think five-feet-four is about the right height?"

"I . . . I'd say she was taller. I saw her legs, and they seemed to be . . . well, they were long legs."

"Slender or chunky?"

"Well formed. I . . . I suppose I should be ashamed of myself, but when that flashlight gave its last flicker of light and showed her lying there, I realized how beautiful a woman's legs can be. I thought there were lots *of* them — the legs I mean."

"You would, under the circumstances," Mason said. "You were standing at her feet and looking up. The legs would look longer under those circumstances. Your best way to estimate her height is how she stood when she was close to you and you were kissing her good night. Was she wearing shoes with fairly high heels?"

"Let me think," Ansley said, frowning.

"Oh-oh!" Mason said. "Here's Della with something important."

Della Street came hurrying toward the table from the phone booth.

"What?" Mason asked as he saw the expression on her face.

"Paul Drake took a short cut on getting the ownership of that automobile," she said. "I told him you were in a hurry so he decided to work through a friend in police headquarters."

"And what happened?" Mason asked.

"CVX 266," she said, "is the license number of a Cadillac sedan that was stolen about two hours ago. The police have broadcast a description, hoping they could pick up the car. It seems it belongs to someone rather important and was stolen from the place where it had been parked at some social function. Quite naturally, when Paul Drake telephoned in and asked for the registration report on a Cadillac, CVX 266, and the man at Headquarters found out that the car was hot and police were trying to locate it, you can imagine what happened."

"In other words, Drake finds himself in a spot," Mason said.

"Exactly," she said.

"What did he do?"

"He told the police that he *thought* the car had been involved in an accident of some sort, that a client of his had telephoned in asking him to check the ownership, that he expected the client to call back again in a short time, at that time Drake would tell the client to report to the police at once."

"The police are satisfied with that?" Mason asked.

"They're not satisfied," she said. "They're accepting it temporarily because they have to. Drake told me he's had trouble enough with the police because of things he's had to do for you in the past, and he doesn't want any more."

Ansley said, "Good heavens! I don't want to have it known I was out there at Borden's. Can't we — ?"

Mason said to Della Street, "Call Paul Drake, tell him he can tell the police that the client he's working for is Perry Mason, that Mason is going to call in after a while, and Drake will tell Mason to report to the police everything he knows about the car. That will put Paul Drake in the clear."

"Where will that leave you?" Della Street asked.

"I'll be all right," Mason said. "I'll report to the police where the car is, but *I* won't tell them the name of *my* client. I'll simply state that I happen to know the car tried to turn into the driveway and was going at too fast a speed and rolled over."

"That wasn't what happened," Ansley reminded Mason. "She was dodging something in the road."

"That's what she told you," Mason said. "Now let's think a little more about that woman who was driving the car. We were talking about shoes. What sort of heels?"

Ansley said thoughtfully, "You suggested she must have been wearing high heels. She wasn't. The shoes were — Say, wait a minute. She must have — She *couldn't* have changed shoes!"

Mason's eyes were level-lidded. "Go on," he said.

"Why, I remember now. I saw one of the shoes when she was lying unconscious. When she got out of the automobile, they weren't the same kind of shoes."

"What do you mean?"

"When she was lying there I saw . . . let's see, I guess it was the right shoe. It was open at the end. You know, open over the end of the toe. But when she got out of the car, her shoes were solid over the toe. She couldn't have had one shoe on one foot and another on another foot, and yet she couldn't have changed shoes. She —"

Mason pushed back his chair from the table. "Come on," he said, "we're going out and take a look at that car."

"At the car?"

"Sure," Mason said. "There were *two* women."

"What!"

"One woman was lying there unconscious," Mason went on. "You saw her, then you started running toward the house and yelling for help. The other girl didn't want that. She must have dragged the unconscious girl to one side, taken her place, assumed the same position of the other girl, then called out for help. When you came back, she gave you just enough of a glimpse so that you would see she was lying in the same position the other person had been. Then she scrambled to her feet, said she was all right, told you she'd been driving the car by herself and asked you to take her home. . . . You said you didn't see her driving license, didn't you?"

"That's right. I remember she laughingly said something about the fact that it was only when people were formal that they were supposed to show their driving licenses and all that, but that we were getting along informally."

"And she let you kiss her in order to show that it *was* informal. I take it, it was an informal kiss?"

"Well," Ansley admitted, "it distracted my

attention from such things as her driving license."

"Come on," Mason told him. "Let's go. I want to see how deep you're into this thing before I start cutting corners.

"Della, ring up Paul Drake. Tell him he can tell the police I am the one who made the inquiry, but have him tell the police that he doesn't know where I can be reached. That will be technically true.

"I'll be getting the car while you're phoning, and we'll run out there and take a look at the situation."

"Then what?" Ansley asked anxiously.

"If that other young woman isn't hurt too badly," Mason said, "you may be able to keep from reporting the accident. If, as I rather suspect may be the case, we find another woman rather badly injured, we're going to have to do some tall explaining and you're going to have to answer a lot of questions."

Chapter 3

The drizzle which had been intermittent during the late afternoon and early evening had settled into a cold, steady rain by the time Mason's headlights picked up the entrance to Meridith Borden's grounds.

"Here you are," Ansley said. "It happened right here. Right inside the gate there. If you'll stop right here, you can see the gap in the hedge."

Mason braked his car to a stop, opened the glove compartment and took out a flashlight.

"Now, we're not going to get caught prowling in the grounds," Mason said. "The first thing is to find out whether my suspicions are correct. If they are, we'll take a quick look for this other young woman who was a passenger in the automobile. If we don't spot her right away, we'll go to Borden's house and then you'll have to notify the police. Do you know much about Meridith Borden?"

"Only his reputation and what little I know from talking with him," Ansley said.

Mason said, "He's supposed to have lots of enemies. This wall topped by broken glass and barbed wire is rather eloquent in itself. I understand that at a certain hour electrically controlled gates are swung shut. Moreover, savage watchdogs can be released to patrol the grounds in case of any alarm. Now, let's stay together, carry on an organized search in an orderly manner and get out of here. First let's take a look at the car. You can show us that."

"The car's right over here, Mr. Mason, through this gap in the hedge."

Mason said to Della Street, "Perhaps you'd better stay in the car, Della. This is going to be wet and muddy and —"

She shook her head emphatically. "You'll need witnesses if you find anything, and if it's a woman, you'll want me along."

She slid across the seat and out of the car.

Ansley led the way through the gate toward the overturned automobile. Mason directed the beam of his flashlight on the pathway, pausing to help Della Street through the tangled, wet, broken branches of the hedge.

"We'll give the place one quick going over," Mason said, "and then we'll know what to do. Where was this young woman lying, Ansley?"

"Right over here on the other side of the car — around this way."

Mason played the beam of the flashlight along the ground.

Abruptly Della Street said, "Someone with heels did a lot of walking around here, Chief."

"Yes," Mason said, "and you can see over here where she was dragging something. She braced herself. Look at those heel marks. She was digging in with her heels."

"Then there *were* two women," Ansley said.

"It looks like it," Mason commented, the beam of his flashlight playing around on the ground.

"She couldn't have dragged the other woman very far," Della Street said. "Not in the brief time she had."

Mason sent the beam of the flashlight in questing semi-circles over the wet grass.

"Well," Mason said at length, "it's pretty certain that this other woman either recovered consciousness and walked off, or else someone came for her and carried her off. In the brief interval that elapsed from the time you left the automobile and started for the house, Ansley, and then returned to find the young woman struggling to a sitting position, a body could hardly have been dragged more than a few yards. Unless, of course, there were three people in the automobile, and one person continued to drag the body over the wet grass while the other one spread herself out to decoy you back."

"Do you think that could have happened?"

"It could have," Mason said, "but I doubt it. In the first place, there are lots of heel tracks in the wet soil there around the automobile, but we don't find any others after that."

"Miss Street isn't making any heel tracks where she's walking," Ansley pointed out.

"Because she's not dragging anything," Mason said. "If she were trying to drag a body, she'd leave tracks."

"So what do I do now?" Ansley asked.

"We'll take a look inside of the automobile, then we'll take one more quick look in the immediate vicinity. If we don't find someone lying here unconscious or wandering around in a dazed condition, we get in the car and you go home and forget it."

Mason turned his flashlight on the interior of the car. "There doesn't seem to be anything there," he said, "and I don't want to leave fingerprints on it, making a detailed search."

He moved the beam of the flashlight around the interior of the car.

"What about the car being stolen?" Ansley asked.

"I'll let Paul Drake tell the police that a client of mine saw a car skid off the road and overturn, that he happened to remember the license number of the car, that it was driven by a young woman who gave the name of Beatrice Cornell, that she said she was unhurt, that he picked her up and took her to her home at the Ancordia Apartments. I'll state that I was consulted simply because my client wanted to know whether it was necessary to report the accident to the police. That will be the truth, perhaps not all the truth, but it covers the essential facts. I'll make it appear a routine matter, and the police may let it drop at that."

"Suppose they don't?"

"Then," Mason said, "I'll protect you as much as I can as long as I can."

"That suits me," Ansley said. "Let's go. This place gives me the willies. I feel shut in."

"Yes," Mason agreed. "Wandering around these grounds at night with a flashlight without permission puts us in a questionable position. We —"

He broke off as an electric gong sounded a strident warning.

"What's that?" Ansley asked apprehensively.

"I don't know," Mason said. "It may be we've set off an alarm. Come on, let's get out of here."

"Which direction is your car?" Ansley asked.

"This way," Mason said. "Now, let's keep together. Della, hang onto my coat. Ansley, keep at my right hand."

A peculiar whirring sound came from the darkness ahead. As they came through the hedge, they heard the clang of metal. The flashlight disclosed that the heavy iron gates had shut. A lock clicked.

"Now what?" Ansley asked in dismay. "We'll have to go to the house to have the gates opened for us."

Mason went to the gates, studied the lock.

Ansley reached for the gates.

"Don't touch them," Mason warned. "There may be a —"

The warning came too late. Ansley pulled at the gates. Almost instantly a siren screamed from someplace in the yard. Big floodlights came on, dispersing the shadows in a blaze of light.

Suddenly they heard the barking of a dog.

"Come on," Mason said, breaking into a run and dashing through the break in the hedge. The others followed his lead.

The brick wall loomed ahead of them.

The barking dog had now been joined by another dog, and the frenzy of barking was drawing unmistakably closer.

"All right," Mason said, "there's only one way out of this fix. Della, we're boosting you

58

up the wall. Help me put her up, Ansley, then I can give you a boost to the top of the wall. Then you can help me up. Here, take off your coat."

Mason whipped off his own coat and threw it up over the broken glass at the top of the wall. Ansley, after a moment, followed suit.

"Come on," Mason said, picking Della Street up in his arms. Then, cupping his hand under her foot, said, "Put a hand on my head, reach up to the top of the wall. Be sure to grab the coat. Straighten your knees. Keep your legs rigid. Up you go."

Mason boosted Della Street up to the wall. "Watch your hands," he warned. "Keep the coats between you and the glass and barbed wire.

"All right, Ansley, you try it. Della, give him a hand. Ansley, put your foot here on my leg. Now get your hip up on my shoulder. Hold your legs rigid as soon as I get hold of your feet and ankles. Then after I've raised you, you can — We're going to have to hurry."

Ansley scrambled up, extended a hand to Della Street.

"Careful now," Mason warned. "Don't pull Della off. Let me give you a shove."

The lawyer pushed Ansley up, then caught his shoes and said, "Straighten your legs now.

That's it! Get hold — All right, quick! You're going to have to grab me — both of you."

Della Street, crouched on the wall, reached down a hand. Ansley did likewise. Mason caught the two hands and jumped. They slowly straightened, pulling the lawyer up to where he could get his feet on the wall. Mason had no sooner reached the top of the wall than a dark object came streaking out of the dazzling light to hurl itself against the wall, leaping almost to the top.

"Doberman pinscher," Mason said, "and he's trained for this sort of stuff. Come on, let's get down on the other side. We lower Della first, Ansley. Then you and I make a jump for it."

The dog was jumping up against the wall, snapping his teeth in an ecstasy of rage, coming within a matter of inches of the feet of the trio as they stood on the wall.

Della Street backed over the edge of the wall. Mason and Ansley lowered her.

"Go ahead, jump," Mason said to Ansley. "It isn't over six feet."

Ansley placed a hand on the folded coats, vaulted to the ground. Mason followed.

"What about your coats?" Della Street asked.

Mason said, "I'll lift you on my shoulders. Try to salvage the coats. You won't be able to keep from tearing them when you pull them loose, but try not to leave enough for evidence. We'll have to hurry! Those confounded lights will make us the most conspicuous objects on the highway."

Mason picked up Della Street. "All right," he said, "straighten your knees, Della. Don't get panicky and don't scratch your hands."

"I can help hold her," Ansley said, "If —"

"No. You get the coats as she hands them down," Mason said. "This is all right. I can hold her."

Della Street worked at the garments. "They're pretty badly tangled on the barbed wire," she said.

"Tear them loose," Mason said, "a car's coming."

The dog continued its frenzied barking from the other side of the wall. Della Street glanced down the highway at the headlights which were coming through the rain-swept darkness, tugged at the coats, got them loose, tossed them to Ansley, then said, "Okay, Chief, I'll slide down."

A moment later she was on the ground.

Mason said, "Get your coat on quick, Ansley. Let's be walking along here and try to look inconspicuous."

The twin headlights became two dazzling eyes. The car swerved, slowed for a moment, then hissed on past, throwing out a stream of moisture which splashed drops on the trio as they stood motionless.

"Let's go," Mason said, "before another car comes."

The lawyer fished the flashlight from his hip pocket, illuminated the way along the shoulder of the road, disclosing a muddy path at the base of the masonry wall.

Della Street took the lead, running lightly. Ansley came behind her, and Mason, holding the flashlight, brought up the rear.

The path followed the wall until it came to the driveway.

Mason said, "Let's have a look at these gates."

"Do we have to do anything more? Can't we just go on?" Ansley asked.

Mason said, "Suppose that other woman who was in the car *didn't* get out of the grounds, but is wandering around the grounds. Think what the dogs will do to her."

"Good heavens!" Della Street said.

Mason said, "In all probability she got out of the grounds, or else she got to the house. However, there's always the probability. Let's — Here's a button."

Mason's flashlight disclosed a call button set in solid cement in the masonry. Over the button was a bronze plaque bearing the words,

PRESS THIS BUTTON THEN OPEN THE DOOR ON THE LEFT. PICK UP THE TELEPHONE AND STATE YOUR BUSINESS.

Mason jabbed his thumb against the button, opened the door of a metallic box imbedded in the cement, picked up a telephone, and held it to his ear.

Seconds elapsed during which he pressed the button repeatedly and listened at the telephone.

Ansley, plainly nervous, said, "Well, we've done all we can."

"You and Della get in the car," Mason instructed. "Get out of the rain. I'll give this another try."

Mason again pressed the button in a series of signals and held the receiver to his ear.

There was a faint buzzing noise on the line, but nothing else.

Ansley hurried to the car. Della Street stood in the rain at the lawyer's side. "Isn't there any other way of reaching the house? Couldn't we —"

A feminine voice came over the telephone. "Hello, yes, what is it, please?" she asked.

Mason said, "There's been an accident. A car is wrecked in your driveway. A young woman may be wandering around the grounds."

"Who are you?" the voice asked.

"We just happened to be passing by," Mason said.

"I'll see what I can do. I don't think Mr. Borden wants to be disturbed, but —"

An abrupt click at the other end of the line indicated she had hung up.

Mason jabbed the button repeatedly.

After a few moments, he said to Della Street, "Take this, will you, Della? Keep jabbing away. Something caused the woman to hang up. She may be calling Borden. I'll get things straightened out in the car."

Della Street put the receiver to her ear, continued to press the button.

Suddenly she said, "Yes, hello."

There was a moment's pause. She looked at Mason, nodded, and said, "Mr. Borden, this is an emergency. We're the party at the gate who reported the auto accident. There's a possibility that a young woman may have been dazed and thrown out of the car, and may still be wandering around the grounds."

There was silence for a few moments, broken only by the squawking noises coming from the receiver in the telephone.

Then, as the receiver ceased making noise, Della Street said with dignity, "I see no reason to give you my name. I'm simply a passer-by."

She hung up.

Mason raised his eyebrows.

"That was Borden himself," she said. "He told me that someone had set off a burglar alarm by tampering with the gates. He said that the burglar alarm automatically releases watchdogs and turns on the floodlights. He's going to call the dogs back into their kennels and switch off the floodlights. He insisted someone had tried to open the gates from the inside. We'd probably better get out of here. I think he'll send someone to investigate."

Mason grabbed Della Street's arm and hurried over to the car.

"Well?" Ansley asked.

"We've done our duty," Mason said. "We've warned them that someone may be inside the grounds. There's nothing more we can do. Let's get out of here. There'll be someone at the gates any second now."

"I'm a mess," Ansley said. "My coat has a tear in it and I'm soaking wet."

Della Street laughed nervously. "Who *isn't* a mess?"

Mason eased the car into gear. "I've got to make up some excuse that will get Paul Drake off the hook as far as that stolen-car report is concerned."

He turned to Ansley. "I'm going to take you back to where you left your car. Get in it and drive home. Don't send your clothes to the cleaners. Take them off, hang them in a closet and forget about them. Say nothing to anyone about what happened. I'll take care of the rest.

"In due course I'll send you a bill for my services."

Mason drove back to the night club. "Okay, Ansley, pick up your car. Go home. Keep quiet. Notify me if anything happens. I think you're in the clear."

Ansley got out in the drizzle. "I'm sure glad I put it in your hands," he said. "You don't think I have to tell the police about the accident?"

"You have to report an accident in which someone was injured," Mason said. "You don't *know* anyone was injured. Moreover, the accident took place on a private driveway, not on a public road."

"Then I don't need to report it?"

"I didn't say that," Mason told him. "I'm simply suggesting that you leave all of that to me."

"That I'll gladly do. Exactly what am I supposed to do now?"

"Get in your car and go home."

Ansley shook hands with Mason and went across to the place where he had parked his car.

Mason said, "All right, Della, I'm driving you home where you can get into some dry clothes, then I'm going up to talk with Paul Drake."

"And what about you?"

"I'll change a little later on."

"Now look, Chief, you're not going to go wondering around in those wet clothes. Paul Drake isn't in such a jam that it can't wait, and I'm going up with you."

"Oh no, you're not."

"Oh yes, I am. I'm going to see that you get into some dry clothes before you start running around. You can drive by my apartment. It'll only take me a minute to change. Then we'll stop at your place on the way to see Paul Drake."

"All right," Mason said after an interval. "Remember what I told Ansley. Don't send any torn clothes to the cleaners. You didn't leave any part of your wearing apparel on the barbed wire, did you?"

"Not of my wearing apparel," she said, "but I'm afraid I left a little skin."

"Where?" Mason asked. "Where were you scratched?"

She laughed. "Where it won't show. Don't worry."

"You'd better get some antiseptic on the places where you're scratched," Mason told her.

"It's all right. I'll take care of it."

Mason drove to Della's apartment.

"Come on up and have a drink," she invited, "while I change. It will at least warm you up a bit."

They went to Della Street's apartment. She opened the door, said, "The liquor is in the closet over the icebox. While I change, get out some water, sugar and nutmeg and you can mix a couple of those hot buttered rums you make so well. I'm so cold the marrow of my bones feels chilly."

"You get into a hot bath," Mason told her. "I'll go see Drake and —"

"No, I'm going to stay with you and see that you get into some dry clothes. Otherwise you'll put off changing until after you've seen Drake. And, for your information, Chief, there's a very nasty, jagged tear in the back of your coat."

"That confounded wall," Mason said. "It certainly was armed to the teeth with barbed wire and broken glass."

"I'll only be a minute," she told him.

"At least take a hot shower," Mason said.

She laughed. "Just get that water hot and use plenty of Bacardi, Chief."

"In yours," he said, "not in mine. When I'm driving I'm sober."

She hurried into the bedroom. Mason went to the kitchenette, fixed a hot buttered rum for Della Street, a hot, black coffee for himself. Ten minutes later they were on the road to Mason's apartment, where the lawyer hurriedly changed into dry clothes. Then he and Della Street went to Paul Drake's office, which was on the same floor of the building where Mason had his offices.

Paul Drake, tall, quizzical and quiet, looked up in annoyance. "It took you two long enough to get here," he said. "The police have given me a bad time. They don't like it."

Mason said, "Go ahead. Get the call through."

Drake sighed with relief, put the call through to the stolen-car department, said, "This is Paul Drake. My client who wanted to know about that car, Number CVX 266, just came in. I'll put him on the line. Here he is now."

Mason took the phone from Drake, said, "Hello. Perry Mason talking. . . . That's right, Perry Mason, the lawyer."

"Now, what's the idea of the lawyer?" the voice at the other end of the line complained. "We're trying to trace a stolen car and we keep getting a run-around."

"No run-around at all," Mason said. "I had a client who called me in connection with an automobile, CVX 266. The car had gone out of control, skidded into a private driveway and turned over. He had picked up the young woman who was driving the car and wanted to know whether he should report the accident to the police."

"Anyone injured?"

"Apparently not."

"That's a stolen car."

"So I understand — now."

"Well, where is it?"

"It's lying in the grounds of Meridith Borden, a public relations expert. He has a country estate about twelve miles out of town, and —"

"I know the place. You mean the one with the wall around it?"

"That's the one."

"And the car's there?"

"That's right."

"Well, it sure took us long enough to get the information," the officer said irritably. "Why didn't you let us know so we could pick up the car?"

"I didn't know it was that important," Mason said. "I just thought it would be a good idea to trace the registration."

"All right. Who's that client of yours?"

"That," Mason said, "is a confidential matter. I can't divulge the name of a client without the client's permission. I can, however, tell you where to recover the automobile, and I have done so."

"Now look here," the officer said, "we're trying to find out about a stolen car, and —"

"And I've told you where the car is," Mason said. "I have no other information I am at liberty to give. You're interested in a car. I'm interested in a client."

Mason hung up the phone.

He grinned at Della Street, said, "Go on home, Paul. If anyone tries to get tough with you, put the blame on my shoulders. I'm going to leave the car parked down here in the parking lot, and Della and I are going down to the Purple Swan, have about three of their hot buttered rums and go home in a taxi. I won't drive when I've been drinking, and I need a drink.

"Get out of here. If you stick around you *may* get —"

Paul Drake lunged for his hat.

"Save the rest of it," he said. "I'm halfway down in the elevator right now."

Chapter 4

Perry Mason latchkeyed the door of his private office, tossed his hat on the shelf of the hat closet, grinned at Della Street and said, "Hi, Della. How did you recover from last night — okay?"

"Okay," she told him.

"No sniffles?"

"No sniffles, no sneezes, no sinuses."

"Good girl."

"Paul Drake telephoned a few minutes ago and said he wanted to have you call just as soon as you came in."

"Give him a ring," Mason said. "The police have probably been giving him a bad time again."

Della Street picked up the telephone, said to the switchboard operator, "Tell Paul Drake Mr. Mason is in now."

Mason lit a cigarette, regarded the pile of mail on his desk with some distaste, pushed it to one side, said, "We haven't heard anything from Ansley this morning, have we?"

"Not a word."

Drake's code knock sounded on the office door.

"Well," Della said, "I guess Paul Drake decided to come down in person."

"That means he wants something," Mason said, grinning. "Open the door, Della, and let's see what it is."

Della Street opened the door, and Paul Drake, his face an unsmiling mask of grave concern, entered the office, said, "Hi, everybody. What the hell were you two doing last night?"

"Now that," Mason said, "has all the earmarks of being an impertinent question."

"I trust you weren't out at Meridith Borden's," Drake said.

"We reported that a car had swerved into Borden's driveway and overturned," Mason said. "Isn't that enough to satisfy the police?"

"You mean you haven't heard?" Drake asked.

"Heard what?"

"It was announced on the radio on the newscast at eight-thirty."

"What was?" Mason asked.

"Meridith Borden, noted public relations expert, was found dead in the palatial residence on his country estate at seven o'clock this morning by his housekeeper. He was lying

73

on the floor in his photographic room and had been shot through the heart, apparently with a revolver."

"Police find any weapon?"

"No weapon, no indication of suicide. On the other hand, no indication of a struggle. However, shortly after eleven o'clock last night a burglar alarm was turned in from the Borden estate, at least from the grounds. Police found indications that some unauthorized persons had been in the grounds and had probably managed to get over the wall."

"Was the burglar alarm connected with police headquarters anywhere?" Mason asked.

"No. A passing motorist heard the siren of the alarm and saw the floodlights go on. Everything was normal at midnight when a sheriff's patrol car made a regular run by the place, so someone must have turned off the lights and reset the alarm.

"The estate is protected by a masonry wall covered with broken glass and barbed wire on top. There are huge iron gates protecting the driveway, and there's an electric timing system by which those gates are automatically closed at eleven o'clock each night. A bell or gong gives a warning sound one minute before the gates close. Then the gates clang shut, and after that the only way anyone can get in is by telephoning from the outer gate."

Mason gave Drake's statement thoughtful consideration.

"What do the police say about it?" Mason asked at length.

"They're not saying anything just yet. They found some tracks in the damp soil around that automobile you reported, indicating that people had been milling around it, evidently looking for something."

"Indeed," Mason said.

"Someone had climbed over the wall," Drake went on. "Some garments had evidently been thrown over the top of the wall covering the broken glass and barbed wire, and then people had climbed over. Police are inclined to think there were three people, and that one of them was a woman."

"How come?" Mason asked.

"Tracks of a woman's heels on both sides of the wall," Drake said, "and the way the police have it worked out, it would have taken a minimum of three people to have scaled the wall. Two people could hardly have done it. A man could have boosted a woman up to the top of the wall, but she couldn't have pulled him up by herself. However, she could have given an assist to another man who was also being helped up from the ground."

"All very interesting," Mason said.

"I thought you might find it *quite* interesting," Drake observed. "Under the circumstances, the police are naturally taking quite an interest in the stolen car which was found overturned on the grounds."

"When did they find the car, by the way?" Mason asked.

"Not until this morning. Police telephoned Borden last night to see if any such car was in the grounds, but there was no answer on Borden's telephone. They sent a squad car out, and, since the gates were closed and the place locked up for the night, they decided to let it wait until morning."

"Any indication as to the identity of the people who were in Borden's grounds last night, Paul?"

"Not yet, Perry. At least, if the police have any evidence, they're not releasing it. Doubtless you'll receive a visit from members of the Homicide Squad this morning. They'll want to ask you more about the client who reported the stolen car careening off the highway."

"Well," Mason said, "that starts the day off with a bang, Paul. I was afraid I was going to be up against a routine morning of answering mail. Thanks for telling me."

"You want me to do anything?" Paul Drake asked.

"Just keep quiet," Mason said.

"I mean along investigative lines."

Mason stretched back in his chair and yawned. "I had met Meridith Borden a couple of times, and, of course, I'm sorry to learn of his tragic demise. But the mere fact that a client reported seeing a car swerve and go out of control into the Borden driveway doesn't give me any interest in the Borden murder."

Drake's face showed unmistakable relief. "Well, thank heavens for that! I was afraid you'd become mixed up in something that could prove embarrassing. There's no chance you, Della and your mysterious client were climbing over Borden's wall last night, is there?"

Mason threw back his head and laughed. "You do a lot of worrying, Paul. What put that idea into your head?"

"The curve of the driveway," Drake said dryly, "is such that a person following a car along the highway might have seen the car swerve into the Borden driveway, but couldn't possibly have seen the car crash through the hedge and then roll over — not without stopping the car, backing up and then walking along the driveway to investigate. There's evidence that quite a number of people were leaving tracks around the Borden driveway. Or, let me put it this way, there's evidence that some people left a lot of tracks. There must have been quite a bit of nocturnal activity, probably prior to eleven o'clock, when the gates were automatically closed by this timing device."

"I see," Mason said thoughtfully.

"And," Drake went on, "in view of the fact that the police are now investigating a murder which may have taken place between nine and eleven o'clock last night, it might be very embarrassing for you to withhold information or to make some statement which you might have to amend at a later date."

"Thanks for the tip, Paul."

"Not at all," Drake said. "You're sure you don't want me to do anything — any investigative work?"

"Not now," Mason said.

"Okay. Keep your nose clean," Drake told him, and heaving his long length from the overstuffed chair, started for the door, paused, looked speculatively at Mason and said, "You know, the police are pretty thorough, Perry. There are times when you think they do dumb things, but once they start after something, they sure as hell keep after it."

"Well?" Mason asked.

"You and Della went out to dinner," Drake said. "I saw you when you left the office building. You were wearing a brown, double-breasted business suit. Della Street had on a

78

dark-blue tailored suit with white trim. When you came into my office to report that an automobile had skidded into Borden's driveway, you were wearing different clothes."

"Do you *always* notice things like that?" Della Street asked.

"It's my business," Paul said. "The point is, Perry, that the police, as I have said, aren't dumb. The fact that they haven't called on you this morning *may* be because they're digging out some facts to work with. They may have found some bits of clothing or some threads stuck to the barbed wires or the broken glass on the Borden wall. It would be just like the police to check on where you had dinner last night, to ask some of the waiters who know you how you were dressed, and then call on you this morning and ask if you'd have any objection to producing the clothes you were wearing last night."

"Why should I have any objection?" Mason asked.

"There might be some significant tears in the cloth."

"And if there were?"

"They might match threads that police found adhering to the barbed wire and the broken glass on top of the wall at Borden's place."

"And if they did?"

"You'd have some explaining to do."

"And if I explained?"

Drake shrugged his shoulders. "It's up to you, Perry. I'm not telling you how to practice law. I'm telling you what the score is."

"Thanks," Mason said. "I'll let you know if I want anything."

"Okay," Drake told him. "Be seeing you."

As soon as Drake had closed the door, Mason nodded to Della Street. "Get Ansley on the phone."

Della Street hurried to the phone book, looked up his number, and said, "Shall I have Gertie at the switchboard dial him, or —"

Mason shook his head. "Try him on our unlisted line, Della. Perhaps it's just as well not to let Gertie know anything about this."

Della Street's nimble fingers dialed the number. After a moment, she said, "Mr. Ansley, please."

She cupped her hand over the mouthpiece, said to Perry Mason, "His secretary wants to know who's calling."

"Tell her," Mason said.

Della Street removed her hand, said into the telephone, "It's Mr. Perry Mason, the attorney, and it's quite important."

There was a moment's silence, then she said, "I see. Will you please tell him when he comes in to get in touch with Mr. Mason, that Mr.

Mason would like to have him call at his earliest convenience. And please tell him that it's a matter of some importance."

She hung up the phone, turned to Mason. "Ansley isn't in. He phoned his office that he wouldn't be in this morning and might not be in all day."

"Didn't leave a number where he could be reached?"

Della Street shook her head. "His secretary said he's undoubtedly out on the job somewhere. There are no phones on those construction projects, and Ansley moves around quite a bit from the jobs to the supply houses. She said that she'd have him call as soon as he came in."

"All right," Mason said, "I guess that determines our pattern for the day, Della."

"What does?" she asked.

"We're out of the office and may not be in all day. I've got to talk to Ansley before I talk with the police."

"How much time do we have before they develop a clue which will lead them here?" Della Street asked.

"That's hard to tell," Mason said. "Remember that my car was parked in front of Borden's wall for a while last night. Someone may have noticed the license number. Remember that we told the police the stolen car was in Borden's grounds and that a client had seen it swerve off the road and roll over, a story which is completely impossible because a motorist couldn't have seen the car after it swerved off the road, and couldn't have known that it rolled over. Put all of these things together in connection with a murder case, and you can gamble that our friends from the Homicide Squad are working on other clues pointing to me, otherwise they would have been here before this."

"And the other clues are?"

"Probably threads torn from our garments. Did you notice Ansley's coat?"

"I know there was a section torn from the lining," she said. "I — Gosh, Chief, I could have been more careful. As it was, I was in a hurry and — well, those barbs seemed to be sticking in every place and I —"

"Sure," Mason said, "you were simply trying to get the clothes free and get away from there as quickly as possible. You had no reason to realize the importance of not leaving threads or bits of cloth. . . . I take it you have some shopping you'd like to do today and perhaps you'd like to spend the afternoon at a beauty parlor, or drop in at a matinee?"

"And in case I'm questioned, what do I say about where I spent the day and how I spent the day?"

"You are entitled to a day off," Mason said. "You've been working overtime."

"When?" she asked.

"That's a good point," Mason told her. "Don't try to cover up. In case you're questioned, say you did quite a bit of work last night."

"And then what?"

"If they ask you anything else, state that you don't answer questioning concerning business matters unless I give you permission."

"Chief, shouldn't I stay with you today?"

Mason shook his head.

"Why not?"

"I don't want to seem to be avoiding the police. If we're together, we would have to be working. If we were working, it would have to be on some case. And if we were working on some case, we might be picked up and questioned before we're ready to be questioned. If, however, you're taking a day off, you can keep yourself out of circulation where the police wouldn't be picking you up."

"And how about you?"

"Well, I'll have to take care of myself," Mason said, grinning. "I think perhaps I can do it."

"If word gets around that they want to question you, they'll be able to pick you up. You're too well known to circulate around the city without leaving a trail."

"I know it," Mason said, "but I don't think they'll announce that they want to question me. That is, they won't give the information to the radio or the press — not just yet."

"Suppose Ansley calls in while we're gone?"

"I don't think he will," Mason said. "He won't unless the police pick him up. Tell Gertie at the telephone that you're taking a day off, that I'm going to be in and out during the day, that if Ansley should telephone, she's to explain to him that I have to see him and that he's to leave a phone number where he can be contacted."

Mason walked over to pick up his hat.

"Be seeing you, Della," he said.

Her eyes were anxious as she watched him out of the door.

Mason got his car from the parking lot, drove some twenty blocks until he was away from the immediate vicinity of his office, found a parking place, went to a drugstore and consulted the telephone directory. He found the number of Beatrice Cornell in the Ancordia Apartments and dialed it.

A woman's voice, sounding calm and impersonal, said, "Yes, hello."

"Minerva?" Mason asked eagerly.

"What number were you calling, please?"

"I want Minerva."

"There's no one named Minerva here."

"Sorry," Mason said, dropped the receiver into its cradle, returned to his car and made time to the Ancordia Apartments.

He found the name of Beatrice Cornell listed as being in Apartment 108.

Mason pressed the buzzer and almost instantly the electric door release sounded.

The lawyer opened the door, walked through a somewhat gloomy lobby, down a corridor, found Apartment 108 and tapped gently on the door.

The door was opened by a woman who said, with crisp, businesslike efficiency, "I'm Miss Cornell — Why, it's Perry Mason!"

Mason bowed. "I called you last night, but I've never met you, have I?"

"Heavens, no! You've never met me. I'm one of your fans. I've followed your cases with the greatest interest. Your picture is very familiar to me. . . . I suppose you want to see me about what happened last night — your phone call. Come in and sit down," she invited.

Mason entered the sitting room of a double apartment, noticed a large, executive desk on which were three telephones. There was a smaller, secretarial desk with a typewriter, a stenographic chair and a considerable amount of typed material.

She caught the surprise in his face and laughed. "I run a sort of catchall service, Mr. Mason. I answer telephones for a whole select list of confidential clients who want to leave night numbers where messages can be taken, yet want a little more personalized service than the average telephone-answering service. For instance, I have several doctors who telephone me when they're out on their evening calls. I keep track of exactly where they are, and, in case of any emergency, know where they can be located in the shortest possible time. I also have a mail service for clients, do a little secretarial work, run a model service, and, all in all, manage to make a living out of odds and ends. In fact, I'm building up a pretty good business."

"Isn't it rather confining?" Mason asked, accepting the chair she indicated.

"Sure, but it's a good living."

"How long have you been doing this?" Mason asked.

"Seven years, and I've built up a very nice business. Before that I was a photographic model. After a while I began to realize that every tick of the clock was undermining my stock in trade. First, I began to put on a little weight here and there, and then I had to start dieting, and . . . well, after a while I saw the light and got out of the business. Now I have a list of models I book for photographers who want professionals.

"But you didn't come here to talk about me, Mr. Mason. I suppose you want to know about last night, and what you're trying to find out is whether I was involved in an automobile accident."

"And I'd like to find out about your models," Mason said.

"That's simple. I used some of my old connections and friendships to build up a model-booking service. I have half a dozen photographic models who let me handle their bookings."

Mason said, "Thanks for your cordiality and co-operation. I hate to be a nasty, suspicious, skeptical audience, but you're talking to an attorney in a matter which may be of some importance.

"A young woman was involved in an automobile accident last night. She was unconscious for a while. She gave your name and this address. My client took her to this apartment house and delivered her here."

"I see," she said thoughtfully. "And you want some assurance that I wasn't the woman?"

He nodded.

"How serious was the automobile accident?"

"One of the cars overturned."

"You say this young woman was injured?"

"She was thrown out and apparently skidded for a ways. She was lying unconscious. Later on, she came to."

"There were bruises?" she asked.

"Probably. On the legs and hips."

"Well, Mr. Mason," she said, "I was here last night. I answered telephones fifty times. I'm here every night. I feel certain I have no information that would help you."

"Do you know Meridith Borden?" Mason asked.

Her eyes narrowed. "Yes. Why?"

"He's dead."

"What!"

"He's dead. The police think he was murdered sometime last night."

"Good heavens!" she exclaimed.

"And," Mason said, "the automobile accident that I refer to is one that took place in the grounds of Meridith Borden's country estate. You remember it was rainy last night. A car skidded off the road, went through the gates, crashed through the hedge, then turned over."

"Does the registration of the car mean anything?" she asked.

"The car was stolen," Mason said.

She was thoughtful for a few moments, then

she said, "Well, I may as well tell you, Mr. Mason. Meridith Borden is — I mean, was . . . a client of mine."

"In what way?"

"He was an amateur photographer. He played around with pin-up art. Sometimes he got models through me."

"Recently?"

"No, not recently. I think that lately he'd made a private deal with some amateur model who wasn't averse to serving cheesecake either for thrills or for cash."

Mason said, "I'm trying to find out who it was who used your name. She was someone who probably knew Borden and she must have known you. She was taller than you, younger than you. She had dark, chestnut hair with brown eyes. She's someone who knows you personally. She came to this apartment house about —"

"About ten o'clock?" Beatrice Cornell interrupted.

"Probably," Mason said.

"I remember that my bell rang," she said, "and I pressed the buzzer releasing the door catch on the outer door. But no one came to my apartment. I didn't think too much of it at the time. Quite frequently you get wrong calls, and —"

"Do you always press the button opening

89

the door without knowing who it is?" Mason asked.

"Oh, sure," she said. "I suppose I should find out, but after all, I'm in business, Mr. Mason. I have two dozen different irons in the fire, and clients drop in to see me, to pick up personal messages or leave instructions, and some of these models —"

"Let's concentrate on the models," Mason interrupted. "Do you have a model of that description?"

"I have some models," she said. "I . . . I don't like to betray the interests of my clients."

Mason said, "I'll try a different approach. I am an amateur photographer. I'm looking for a model. I don't want one of the slender, long-legged models, I want one with curves. A good figure but well curved. Could you put me in touch with one of your models?"

"I have some sample photographs," she said. "I could show you those."

"Please," Mason said.

She smiled and said, "This is strictly business. These girls will want twenty dollars an hour. They'll want pay from the time they leave their apartment until they return. You'll have to furnish the transportation. You'll have to furnish any special costumes you may want. You'll have to see that they're fed. They have stock costumes. Bikini bathing suits. Some of them want chaperons. Some of them will take a chance if they know you. Some of them will take a chance, period."

"Do I get photographs and addresses?" Mason asked.

"You do not," she said. "You get photographs with numbers on them. My addresses are my stock in trade. I get a commission on any booking. Most of the specimen photographs are in bikini bathing suits."

"That's fine," Mason said. "Let's take a look."

She said, "Just a minute," and went through a door to an adjoining room. Mason heard the sound of the drawer in a filing case opening and closing.

A moment later she was back with a dozen eight-by-ten glossy photographs of good-looking girls in attractive poses. Each photograph had a number pasted to it.

Mason regarded the photographs thoughtfully, eliminated several, said, "I'd like studio appointments with numbers six, eight and nine."

"It'll cost you twenty dollars an hour."

Mason nodded.

She opened an address book.

Abruptly Mason said, "Wait a minute, Miss Cornell. I have a better idea. Ring up every one of your models on the list, ask if they're free today and ask if they can pose for a series of bathing beauty pin-up pictures. And, of course, please understand that I want to pay for your time, whatever it's worth."

"All right," she said. "Sit down and make yourself comfortable. I'll get busy on the phone."

Beatrice Cornell struck pay dirt on the third telephone call. She said, "Just a minute, dearie, I'll . . . well, I'll call you back."

She hung up the telephone, turned to Perry Mason.

"That's Dawn Manning," she said, "an attractive girl with a beautiful torso, pretty well upholstered, an awfully good scout. She says she's out of business for four or five days on account of some rather unsightly bruises. She says she was badly shaken up last night in a minor automobile accident."

"That's my girl," Mason said.

"What do you want to do?"

"Could you get her to come out here?"

"She said she can't pose."

"Tell her," Mason said, "that I've seen her photographs, I like her looks, that we can probably cover up the bruises so they won't show. Ask her if she'll come out here and meet me. Tell her she gets paid from the time she leaves her apartment. Tell her to jump in a taxi and come out."

Beatrice Cornell frowned. "She's going to feel that I've double-crossed her."

"You haven't double-crossed her at all," Mason said. "You're booking photographic models. I've heard of your services. You don't need to mention that I'm an attorney. I'm simply Mr. Mason, a photographer. Ask her to come out here for an interview. Tell her you have the money."

Beatrice Cornell hesitated, said, "Well, I guess it's all right."

Mason took his wallet from his pocket, took out a twenty and a ten. "There's thirty dollars," he said. "Twenty dollars for an hour of her time, and the balance will cover taxi fares and incidental expenses."

"What are you going to do?" she asked. "Are you going to tell this girl who you are and what you want?"

"That depends," Mason said.

"You're going to be a photographer?"

Mason nodded.

"Then you'd better get yourself a camera."

"Is there a photographic store near here?"

"One about four blocks from here. I'm in close touch with him. Want me to telephone?"

"No," Mason said, "I'd prefer you didn't. I'll walk in and get an outfit. I'll have a chance to get back here by the time your girl arrives?"

"Probably. It might be a little better for you to let me talk with her first, and —"

"That's fine," Mason said. "I'll be back in half an hour."

Chapter 5

Thirty minutes later Mason returned to Beatrice Cornell's apartment. He was armed with a twin-lens camera, a Strobolite, a leather carrying case and a dozen rolls of film, both color and black and white.

Dawn Manning was there ahead of him.

Beatrice Cornell performed the introductions.

Dawn Manning's slate-gray eyes appraised the evident newness of Mason's photographic equipment.

"You're an amateur, Mr. Mason?"

He nodded.

"Rather a new amateur, I would say."

Again Mason nodded.

"What is it you want, Mr. Mason?"

"I want some shots," Mason said, "of a model. I'd like to try some . . . well, some . . . well, some —"

"Pin-ups?"

Mason nodded.

She pulled the tight-fitting sweater even

more closely to the contours of her body. "I have nice breasts," she said, "and my legs are good. You understand about my rates?"

"He understands," Beatrice Cornell said.

Dawn met Mason's eyes frankly. "If you're looking for a woman," she said, "go get someone else. If you're looking for photographs, that's different. We don't have trouble with the professionals or the experienced photographers who are accustomed to hiring models. We do have lots of trouble with amateurs, and I don't want trouble."

"Mr. Mason is all right," Beatrice Cornell interposed quickly. "I told you that, Dawn."

"I know you told me that, but . . . well, I just don't want to have any misunderstanding, that's all."

Mason said, "I am willing to pay your rates and I assure you, you won't have to fight me off."

"All right," Dawn Manning said crisply, after a moment's hesitation, "but it'll be a few days before you're able to take shots showing my legs."

"You were in an automobile accident?" Mason asked.

She nodded, said, "I got out lucky at that."

Mason took a cigarette case from his pocket. "Is it all right if I smoke?" he asked.

"Certainly," Beatrice Cornell said.

Dawn Manning took one of Mason's cigarettes.

Mason held a match. Dawn Manning inhaled deeply, held the smoke in her lungs for a moment, then exhaled.

She settled back in the chair, started to cross her legs, then suddenly winced.

"How bad is it?" Mason asked.

"Frankly," she said, "I didn't look at myself in the mirror this morning. I was sleeping late. When Beatrice called, I jumped up, piled into some clothes and came on over."

"Without breakfast?"

She laughed. "I have to watch my weight. Breakfast and I are strangers. Let's take a look and see how things are coming."

She got up from the chair, and, as freely and naturally as though she had been making an impersonal appraisal of a piece of statuary, raised her skirts almost waist-high and examined her left hip. "That's where it's the most tender."

Beatrice Cornell said, "Gosh, Dawn, that would take a *lot* of retouching. It's bad now and by tomorrow it'll be worse."

Dawn Manning kept twisting around trying to look at herself, said, "I feel like a puppy chasing its tail. Let me take a look in that full-length mirror, Beatrice."

She crossed over to stand in front of a door

which contained a panel mirror, and shook her head dolefully as she surveyed herself. "It's worse than it was last night when I went to bed. I'm afraid I'm not going to be available for a few days, Mr. Mason. Will this wait, or do you want another model? I'm sorry. Under the circumstances, I'll only charge you taxi fare."

Mason said, "I think we could arrange things with the proper lighting. . . . Could we go to your apartment? I'd like to have a couple of hours of your time."

Dawn Manning's face flushed. "You certainly can not," she said, "and I'm going to be frank with you, Mr. Mason. I don't work with amateurs without a chaperon. If you're married, bring your wife along. If you aren't married, I'll arrange a chaperon. It's going to cost you three dollars an hour extra."

"All right," Mason told her. "We're chaperoned here. Let's talk here."

"About what? About photographs?"

Mason shook his head. "I may as well confess. I was interested in the bruises."

"In the *bruises?*"

"I wanted to see the nature and extent of your bruises."

"Say, what is this, anyway? What kind of a goof are you?"

"I'm a lawyer."

"Oh-oh," Beatrice Cornell interposed.

"All right, so you're a lawyer," Dawn Manning said indignantly. "You've got me out of bed and up here under false pretenses. You —"

"Not under false pretenses, exactly," Mason interrupted. "I told you I was willing to pay for your time. Miss Cornell has the money."

Dawn Manning's face softened somewhat.

"What is it you want, Mr. Mason? Let's put the cards on the table and see how our hands stack up."

Mason said, "I was interested in your bruises because I am interested in the automobile accident which took place last night."

"Are you intending to sue somebody?"

"Not necessarily. I would like to have you tell me about it. And, since we're taking up Miss Cornell's time without payment, I suggest that we go someplace where we can talk and let her get ahead with her work, or that I make arrangements to compensate *her* for her time."

"And you don't want pictures?" Dawn Manning asked.

"Yes, I want pictures."

"It's all right if you want to talk here," Beatrice Cornell said. "I get a commission on this job, you know, and I —"

"You'll do better than that," Mason told her. "You'll get twenty dollars an hour for *your* time, as well as the commission."

Mason arose, opened his billfold once more, took out sixty dollars and said, "I'll probably use up two hours of your time, first and last, and here's another twenty for Miss Manning."

"Well now, look, that's not necessary, Mr. Mason. I —"

"You have a living to make, the same as anyone else," Mason told her.

"What do you want from me?" Dawn Manning asked.

"First I'd like to know all about the automobile accident," Mason said.

"Well, there wasn't much to it. I went to a studio party last night. A photographer friend of mine was showing some of his pictures and he invited a group of us in for cocktails followed by a buffet dinner. Ordinarily I wouldn't have gone, but he had some pictures of which he was quite proud. I'd been the model and I hadn't seen the proofs. I was interested and he was terrifically proud of his work.

"Quite frequently, at a time like that, a model picks up new business and new contacts, and it's nice to be out with your own kind. Most people who learn you're a photographic model and are willing to pose in bikini bathing suits or without them, under proper circumstances, get the idea you're cheap and that everything you have is for sale.

"However, when you're out with a crowd that knows the ropes and understands each other, you can have a good time and . . . well, it's a nice, free-and-easy professional atmosphere. Everyone respects the work the other one is doing. We like good photography and we like good photographers. They need models to stay in business, and we need photographers to keep us going."

"All right," Mason said, "you went to this party."

"And," she said, "because I wanted to go home early, I went alone. I didn't have an escort and took a taxi. I had some drinks, I had a buffet dinner, I saw the pictures, and they were darned good pictures. He'd used a green filter, which is about as kind to the human skin as anything you can get for black-and-white photography, and the pictures came out nice. As I said, I wanted to get home early, so I broke away before things got to a point where the drinks began to take effect. I was looking for a taxicab when this woman pulled up to the curb in a nice Cadillac and said, 'You were up at the studio party. I saw you there. It's a rainy night. You'll have a hard time getting a cab. Want a ride?'

"I didn't place her, but she *could* have been there. There must have been fifty people in the place altogether at cocktail time. I think only ten or twelve were invited to stay for dinner."

"So you got in with this woman?"

"I got in with this woman and she started driving toward town."

"Did you get her name?"

"I didn't. I'm coming to that. She chatted with me as though we were old friends. She knew my name, where I lived and all that.

"She told me it was a rainy night, that I'd have trouble getting a cab, and that was the reason she'd asked me to ride with her. She said that she had to make one brief stop on the road home."

"This cocktail party was here in town?"

Dawn Manning shook her head. "Out in Mesa Vista," she said. "This whole story is a little weird, Mr. Mason. To understand it you'll have to know a little about my background. I'll have to tell you some of my personal history."

"Go ahead," Mason told her, his eyes narrowing slightly, "you're doing fine."

"I've been married," she went on, "Dawn Manning is my maiden name. I took it after we split up. My ex-husband is Frank Ferney. He's associated with Meridith Borden. He's a chiseler. When we split up, I couldn't go to Reno to get a divorce. Frank agreed to go.

He wrote me he'd filed papers, and I made an appearance so as to save problems of serving summons. I thought everything had been taken care of.

"I don't know how much you know about Meridith Borden. He makes his living out of selling political influence. I did some posing for him. I met a local politician, the politician fell for me, and Borden wanted to use me just as he'd used some party girl to get this politician to the point where — well, where Borden could get something on him.

"I hate these man-and-wife feuds where people are intimate for years and then suddenly start hating each other. My ex-husband wasn't what I thought he was, but I had tried to keep friendly with him.

"This Borden deal was too much. I told them both off. I told the amorous politician he'd better do his playing around at home, and I walked out on the lot of them.

"Well, last night we drove along the road. and this woman said she wanted to turn in to see a friend very briefly. Then she mentioned casually that someone had told her that my husband and I had planned a divorce but that he had not gone through with it. About that time she started to swing into Meridith Borden's driveway. I sensed a trap and grabbed at the wheel to keep her from turning in. We met another car coming out of the driveway. I guess I shouldn't have grabbed at the wheel, but I wasn't going to let them trap me. Anyway, we went into a skid."

"Go on," Mason said, "what happened?"

"We went completely around. I know the other car hit us because I felt the bump, or perhaps I should say we hit the other car. Then I have a recollection of crashing through a hedge and the next I knew I was lying on the damp grass on my left hip with my skirts clean up around my neck as though I had skidded or been dragged some little distance. I was lying in a cold drizzle and I was wet and chilled.

"I moved around a bit, trying to find where I was and thinking what had happened, and finally recollection came back to me all at once. I tested myself to see if I had any broken bones. Apparently, all that I had was a bruised and skinned fanny. I was lying up against the stone wall that surrounds Borden's place. The car I had been riding in was on its side. I looked around for the other woman. She was nowhere around. I was cold, wet and shaken up. I found my way to the driveway, walked through the gates to the highway. After a while a motorist stopped. I hitchhiked to town."

"Do you know this motorist?"

"No, I don't. I didn't get his name and I

didn't want his name. He had an idea he could furnish me board and lodging for the night and was rather insistent. I didn't tell him anything about myself or my background. I let him think I was walking home from a ride during which I'd had an argument with my boy friend.

"As Beatrice can tell you, in this business we get so we can handle ourselves with most men, turn them down and still leave them feeling good. But this particular specimen was a little hard to handle. However, I put up with things until I got to where I could get a bus. Then I slapped his face good, got out, and removed the dollar bill I always keep fastened to the top of my stocking. I took a bus to the corner nearest my apartment and then had to ring the manager to get a duplicate key. I'd lost my purse and everything in it — cigarettes, lipstick, keys, driving license, the works."

"Did you look for your purse?"

"I felt around in the car and on the ground. I couldn't find it. Evidently this woman took it with her."

"What time was this?" Mason asked. "Can you fix the time?"

"I can fix the time of the accident very accurately."

"What time was it?"

"Three minutes past nine."

"How do you know?"

"My watch stopped when I hit the ground, or when I hit the side of the car or something. In any event, the watch stopped and hasn't been running since."

"Do you know what time it was when you left the grounds?"

"I can approximate that."

"What time?"

"I would say about twenty-five minutes before ten. I arrived home at perhaps fifteen minutes past ten, I think. Why? Does it make any great difference?"

"It may make quite a difference," Mason said.

"Would you mind telling me why, Mr. Mason?"

"Unfortunately, I'm a one-way street as far as information is concerned at the moment. I can receive but I can't give. There's one other thing I want. I want the best possible description you can give of the woman who picked you up and gave you a ride in that car."

"Mr. Mason, you're putting me though quite a catechism here."

"I'm paying for your time," Mason reminded her.

"So you are," she said, laughing. "Well, this

106

woman was somewhere in the late twenties, or say, on a guess, around thirty. She was about my height . . . oh, say around five-feet-five, and she weighed . . . well, from 116 to 120, somewhere in there. She had reddish hair, the dark, mahogany type of red that —"

"Comes out of a bottle?" Mason asked.

"Comes in a hair rinse of some sort. I have an idea she might have been a natural brunette."

"What can you remember about her eyes?"

"I remember her eyes quite well because she had a peculiar habit of looking at me, and when she did, it gave me rather an uneasy feeling. Her eyes were dark and . . . it's hard to describe, but there's a sort of a reddish, dark eye that doesn't seem to have any pupil at all. I suppose if you looked carefully enough you could find a pupil, but the color of the eyes is dark and sort of reddish, and you just don't see any pupil."

"You remember that?"

She nodded.

"Anything else?"

"She wore rings on both hands, I remember that. Diamonds. Fairly good-sized stones, too."

"How was she dressed?"

"Well, as I remember it, she didn't have

any hat on and her coat was a beige color, rather good-looking. She had a light wool dress in a soft green that went well with her coloring."

"You hadn't seen this woman before?"

"You mean to know her?"

"Yes."

"No. I'm quite certain I haven't."

Mason glanced at Beatrice Cornell.

Beatrice Cornell slowly shook her head. "There's something vaguely familiar about the description, Mr. Mason, but I don't place it — at least at the moment."

"All right," Mason said. "I guess that covers the situation at the moment. I'd like some pictures."

"Bruises and all?" Dawn Manning asked, laughing.

"Bruises and all — particularly the bruises."

"Okay. We'll throw in the all," Dawn Manning said. "Beatrice can show you how to work that Strobolite.

"Pull the shades, Beatrice, and we'll get to work."

Chapter 6

The cafeteria was a small, cozy place that featured home cooking.

Perry Mason, moving his tray along the smoothly polished metal guide, selected stuffed bell peppers, diced carrots, fried eggplant, pineapple-cottage-cheese salad and a pot of coffee. He moved over to a table for two by the window and settled himself for a leisurely lunch.

A shadow formed back of Mason's shoulder. A man's voice said, "Is this seat taken?"

Mason said somewhat irritably, "No, it's not taken, but there are half a dozen empty tables over there."

"Mind if I sit down?"

Mason looked up in annoyance to encounter the eyes of Lt. Tragg of the Metropolitan Homicide Department.

"Well, well, Tragg," Mason said, getting up and shaking hands as Tragg put his tray down on the table. "I didn't know *you* ate here."

"First time I've ever eaten here," Tragg said. "They tell me the food's pretty good."

"It's wonderful home cooking. How did you happen to find the place?"

"*Modus operandi*," Tragg said.

"I don't get you."

"So many people don't," Tragg said, putting a cup of consommé, some pineapple-cottage-cheese salad and a glass of buttermilk on the table.

Mason laughed. "You don't sample the cooking here by eating that combination, Tragg. The stuffed bell peppers are wonderful."

"I know, I know," Tragg said. "I eat to keep my waistline down within reason. About the only pleasure I get out of being around good cooking is to have the aroma in my nostrils."

"Well," Mason said, as Tragg seated himself, "tell us about the *modus operandi*, Lieutenant."

"I don't know whether you remember the last time you disappeared or not," Tragg said. "It was in connection with a case where you didn't want to be interviewed. And after you finally showed up and got into circulation, you may remember that I asked you where you had been and what the idea was in running away."

110

"I remember it perfectly," Mason said, "and I told you that I hadn't run away."

"That's right," Tragg said. "You told me you had been out interviewing some witnesses and that quite frequently when you did that, you didn't go back to the office but had lunch at a delightful little cafeteria where they featured home cooking."

"Did I tell you that?" Mason asked.

"You did," Tragg said, "and I asked you about the cafeteria. So then I went back to the office, took out my card marked 'Perry Mason, Attorney at Law' and on the back of it under *modus operandi* made a note, 'When Perry Mason is hiding out, he's pretty apt to eat at the Family Kitchen Cafeteria.'

"For your information, Mr. Mason, that's what we call *modus operandi*. It's something we use in catching crooks. Unfortunately, the police can't stand the strain of being brilliant and dashingly clever, so they have to make up for it by being efficient.

"You'd be surprised what we can do with the *modus operandi* filing system of ours and compiling a lot of notes. It may be that a man has certain peculiar eating habits. He may call for a certain brand of wine with his meals. He may like to have a sundae made by putting maple syrup on ice cream. All of those little things that the brilliant, flashy geniuses don't have to bother with, the plodding police have to note and remember.

"Now, take in your case. You're brilliant to the point of being a genius, but the little old *modus operandi* led me to you when we were looking for you, when you didn't want to be found."

"What makes you think I didn't want to be found?" Mason asked.

Tragg smiled and said, "Oh, I presume you were out interviewing witnesses again."

"That's exactly what I was doing," Mason said.

"Are you finished?"

"With the witnesses?"

"Yes."

"No."

"Well," Tragg said, "that's fine. Perhaps I can be of some help."

"And then again perhaps you couldn't," Mason said.

"All right, we'll look at it the other way," Tragg said. "Perhaps *you* could be of some help to *me*."

"Are you seeking to retain my services?"

Tragg sipped the buttermilk, poked at the cottage cheese salad with his fork and said, "Damn, but that stuffed bell pepper smells good!"

"Go on," Mason said, "go on and get yourself a stuffed bell pepper. It will make the world look brighter."

Tragg pushed back his chair, picked up his check, said, "You've made a sale, Perry."

Tragg returned carrying a tray on which were two stuffed bell peppers, a piece of apple pie, a slab of cheese and a small jar of cream.

He seated himself at the table, said, "Now, don't talk to me until I get these under my belt and get to feeling goodnatured once more."

Mason grinned at him, and the two ate in silence.

After he had finished, Tragg pushed his plate back, took a cigar from his pocket, cut off the end with a penknife, said, "I feel human once more. Now let's get down to brass tacks."

"What kind of brass tacks?" Mason asked.

"Arrange them any way you want," Tragg said. "If you put the heads down, the points are going to be up and that's going to be tough — on you."

"What do you want to know?"

Tragg said, "Meridith Borden was murdered. You were out there. You climbed over a wall and set off a burglar alarm. Then, like a damn fool, you didn't report to the police. Instead, you make yourself 'unavailable,' and Hamilton Burger, our illustrious district attorney, wants to have a subpoena issued and drag you in before the Grand Jury, accompanying his action with a fanfare of trumpets."

"Let him drag," Mason said.

Tragg shook his head. "In your case, no, Perry."

"Why?"

"Because you're mixed up in too many murder cases where you're out on the firing line. You aren't content to sit in your office the way other people do and let the evidence come to you. You go out after it."

"I like to get it in its original and unadulterated form," Mason told him.

"I know how you feel, but the point is you have to look at these things from the standpoint of other people. Why didn't you come to us and tell us about the murder?"

"I didn't know about it."

"Says you."

"Says me."

"What were you doing out there?"

"If I told you," Mason said, "you'd think I was lying."

Tragg puffed contentedly at his cigar. "Not me. I might think you'd play hocus-pocus with the district attorney, I might think you'd juggle guns if you had a chance, or switch evidence. You have the damnedest quixotic idea of protecting a client, but you don't lie."

Mason said, "I was peacefully eating dinner,

114

minding my own business. A man came to me and told me he'd been involved in an automobile accident. He had reason to believe someone might have been injured. I went out to the scene of the accident with him, and, while I was there inside the grounds, the iron gates clanged shut. Apparently, they were activated by some sort of a time mechanism. It was exactly eleven o'clock."

"That's right," Tragg said. "There's an automatic timing device that closes the gates at eleven o'clock."

"So we were trapped," Mason said. "Moreover, a nice, unfriendly Doberman pinscher started trying to tear out the seat of my trousers."

Tragg's eyes narrowed. "When?"

"While we were trapped inside. We worked our way along the wall to the gate; the gate was locked tight. There were spikes on top of the gate, and we couldn't climb over it. Somehow we triggered an alarm. Dogs started barking and coming toward us. We got over the wall."

"Who's we?"

"A couple of people were with me."

"Della Street was one," Tragg said.

Mason said nothing.

"The other fellow probably was a contractor by the name of George Ansley," Tragg observed.

Again Mason was silent.

"And you didn't know Borden had been killed?"

"Not until this morning."

"All right," Tragg said. "You've been out hunting witnesses. What witnesses?"

"Frankly, I was trying to find the driver of the automobile that had turned over in the Borden grounds."

"You had Paul Drake looking for that last night. The car was stolen."

"So I understand."

"You're not offering me much information."

"I'm answering questions."

"Why don't you talk and *then* let me ask the questions?"

"I prefer it this way."

Tragg said impatiently, "You're playing hard to get, Mason. You're letting me drag everything out of you. The idea is that you aren't trying to tell me what you know, but are trying to find out how much or how little I know so you can govern yourself accordingly."

"From my standpoint," Mason asked, "what would you do?"

"In this case," Tragg said, "I'd start talking."

"Why?"

"Because," Tragg told him, "whether you're aware of it or not, I'm giving you a break. When I get done talking with you, I'm going to move over to that telephone, call Homicide and tell them that there's no need to get a subpoena for Perry Mason, that I've had a very nice, friendly chat with him and he's given me his story."

Mason's face showed slight surprise. "You'd do that for me?" he asked.

"I'd do that for you," Tragg said.

"This isn't a gag?"

"It's not a gag. What the hell do you think I'm here for?"

"Sure," Mason said, "you're here, but you've got a couple of plain-clothes men scattered around. And, by the time the D.A. releases the story to the newspapers, it will be to the effect that Perry Mason was run to earth by clever detective work on the part of Lt. Tragg of the Homicide Squad."

"I'm handing it to you straight," Tragg said. "I looked at your *modus operandi* card, I got the name of this caferia, I felt there was a chance you'd be here, I came out entirely on my own. No one knows where I am. I simply said I was going out to lunch. As far as I know, there isn't a plain-clothesman within a mile."

Mason studied Tragg's face for a moment, then said, "If you have any information that

117

will give you the identity of my client, you'll have to rely on that. I'm not going to admit the identity of my client right at the moment. I'll tell you the rest of it.

"Della Street and I were having dinner. It was a little after ten o'clock. This man came up to us, he told us that an hour earlier a car had swung past him and overturned in the grounds of Meridith Borden, that the license number was CVX 266, that it had apparently been driven by a young woman who was injured.

"He had a flashlight. As it turned out, the batteries were on their last legs. He got out and walked around the front of the overturned car. He found a woman who had evidently been thrown out and had skidded along on the wet grass. He was looking at lots of legs. She was still alive but unconscious. He didn't dare to move her because he knew that might not be the thing to do. He started toward the house and then heard a call for help behind him. He turned and groped his way back through the darkness. Apparently, the woman had regained consciousness. He helped her to her feet, she said there were no bones broken, she was bruised, that was all, and suggested he drive her home.

"He drove her home. That is, he drove her to the address she gave.

"After I questioned him about it, and he began to think things over, there were things that made me suspicious there might have been *two* young women in the car, that when my client started toward the house the other passenger, who may or may not have been the driver of the car, had pulled the unconscious woman along the wet grass into a position of concealment against the wall, and then had taken her place and had started calling for help."

"Why?" Tragg asked.

"Apparently so my client wouldn't go up to the house."

Tragg took the cigar out of his mouth, inspected the end with thoughtful concentration, then returned the cigar, puffed on it a few times, slowly nodded his head, and said, "That might check. What did you do this morning?"

Mason said, "I tried to find out who the young woman was."

"What did you find out?"

"I went to the address where my client had left her."

"What was the address?"

Mason thought for a moment, then said, "The Ancordia Apartments. The woman had given him the name of Beatrice Cornell. There was a Beatrice Cornell registered. She's some kind of a talent agent and has a telephone-

119

answering service. A lot of people know about her and she has a lot of clients. She says she wasn't out of the apartment yesterday evening, and I'm inclined to believe her."

"Go ahead," Tragg said.

Mason said, "I came to the conclusion that this young woman had given the name of Beatrice Cornell, that she had gone to the apartment house where she knew Beatrice Cornell lived, had rung Beatrice Cornell's doorbell so as to be admitted, had kissed my client good night, then —"

"That cordial already?" Tragg interrupted.

"Be your age, Lieutenant," Mason said.

Tragg grinned. "That's the trouble, I am. Go ahead."

"She went in the apartment house, seated herself in the lobby, waited until my client had driven away, then called a cab and left the place."

"So what did you do?"

"I got Beatrice Cornell to show me her list of pin-up models — girls who rent themselves out at twenty dollars an hour to art photographers."

"In the nude?" Tragg asked.

"I would so assume," Mason said. "Not from the models, but from some of the calendars I've seen. However, it's legal and artistic. They're nude but not naked, if you get what I mean."

"It's always been a fine distinction as far as I'm personally concerned," Tragg said, "but I know the law makes it. Go on, what happened?"

"I found a young woman who seemed to answer the description."

"How?"

"By a process of elimination."

"Such as what?"

Mason grinned and said, "Looking for a girl with a bruised hip."

"Well, that's logic," Tragg said. "You make a pretty damned good detective for a lawyer. What happened?"

"I got this young woman to come out to Beatrice Cornell's apartment. I paid her for two hours' time and her taxi fare. I asked her questions and she told her story."

"Which was?"

"That she had been at a party, that she had gone alone and was planning to return via taxi-cab, that when she went to the curb to pick up a cab, the party who was driving this Cadillac with the license number CVX 266 pulled in to the curb, seemed to know her by name, and acted as though they had met. This woman offered the girl, Dawn Manning, a ride home. She accepted it.

"The woman driving the car said she wanted to stop just for a moment to leave something

121

with a man she knew, and started to turn into Borden's driveway. Another car was coming out —"

"Your client's?" Tragg asked sharply.

Mason said doggedly, "I'm giving you Dawn Manning's story. She said a car was coming out; that she had known Meridith Borden and didn't like his style; that her ex-husband was associated with Borden; that apparently they had wanted to use her in some sort of a badger game to trap a politician; for that reason her husband had delayed finishing up the divorce action. Dawn Manning wouldn't go for it, so naturally she didn't want to be taken into the Borden place; she pulled at the wheel; the Cadillac went into a spin, skidded, grazed the bumper of the other car, crashed through the hedge and that was all she remembered.

"She became conscious, perhaps thirty minutes later, tried to orientate herself, found the overturned car, made her way out to the highway, and —"

"Gates open at that time?" Tragg asked.

"Gates open at that time," Mason said. "She hitchhiked home. That's her story."

"You think it's true?"

"It checks with my theory."

"All right. What about this woman who was driving the car, the one your client took to the Ancordia Apartments?"

"I feel that woman must have known Beatrice Cornell more or less intimately."

"Why?"

"She knew her name, she knew her address, and, in some way, she knew some of the models that Beatrice Cornell had listed. It must have been because of that knowledge that she knew Dawn Manning."

Tragg thoughtfully puffed at his cigar.

"What have you done about locating this other woman — provided Dawn Manning is telling the truth?"

"Dawn Manning has to be telling the truth," Mason said. "She doesn't fit the description given by my client of the young woman he drove home — at least I don't think she does."

"And what have you done about locating the other woman?"

"Nothing yet. I'm thinking."

"All right, let's quit thinking and act."

"What do you mean, let's?"

"You and me," Tragg said.

Mason thought that over for a moment.

"You know," Tragg said, studying Mason over the tip of his cigar, "you're acting as though you had some choice in the matter."

"Perhaps I do," Mason said.

"Maybe you don't," Tragg told him.

"We're taking over now. What you apparently don't realize is the fact that I'm giving you an opportunity to come along as a passenger and take a look at the scenery."

"Okay," Mason told him, "let's go."

Tragg pushed back his chair, walked over to the telephone booth, dialed a number, talked for three or four minutes, then came back to join Perry Mason.

"All right," he said, "you're clean."

"Thanks," Mason said.

"What's more," Tragg said, "we're not going to be trying to pick up Della Street. We *are* going to talk with George Ansley."

"How does Ansley's name enter into the picture?" Mason asked.

Tragg grinned. "When he put his coat over the barbed wire on that wall, part of the lining tore out. It was the part that had a tailor's label in it. You couldn't have asked for anything better. All we had to do was read the guy's name and address, then match the torn lining with the lining that the tailor knew had been put into his coat."

"Simple," Mason said.

"All police work is simple when you come down to it. It's just dogged perseverance."

"Want to go see Beatrice Cornell?" Mason asked.

"Why?"

"Because she must have a clue somewhere in her list of clients. This woman, whoever it was, must know Beatrice Cornell pretty well and is probably a client."

"Could be," Tragg said. "We're trying the simple ways first."

"What's that?"

"Combining all the taxi companies," Tragg said. "After all, we've got the location, the Ancordia Apartments. We've got the time, probably a little before ten. The guy got in touch with you a few minutes past ten, and you went out there and did some running around before the gates closed. What time do you suppose you got there?"

"I would say that we must have arrived around ten minutes before eleven. We were there about that long before the gates closed, and, as I remember it, the gong sounded and the gates closed right at eleven o'clock."

"Right," Tragg said. "Okay, we've got the time. Police are searching taxi calls. There's a phone booth in the lobby of the Ancordia Apartments. It's almost a cinch this babe went inside, waited just long enough to see Ansley drive off, then stuck a dime in the telephone and called a cab.

"What do you say we go on down to my car? I've got a radio on it and I'll get in touch with Communications. They'll have the information for me by the time we're ready to go."

Mason said thoughtfully, "There's a lot of advantage being a police officer."

"And a hell of a disadvantage," Tragg said. "Come on, let's go."

Chapter 7

The loud-speaker on Lt. Tragg's car crackled:

"Calling Car XX-Special. Calling Car XX-Special."

Tragg picked up the mouthpiece, said, "Car XX-Special, Lieutenant Tragg."

The voice replied, "Go to telephone booth and call Communications. Repeat, telephone booth, call Communications. Information party desired now available."

"Will call," Tragg said, and dropped the transmitter back on the hook. He grinned at Mason and said, "That means they've located something. They don't want it put out on the general communications system. They —"

Tragg glanced swiftly behind him and swung the car into a service station where a telephone booth was located at the back of the lot.

"Sit here and hold the fort, Perry," he said. "If a call comes in for XX-Special, just pick up the receiver and state that Lieutenant Tragg is calling Communications on a telephone circuit and any message can be sent to him there."

Tragg hurried into the phone booth, and Mason could see him talking, then taking notes.

Tragg hung up the phone, returned to the car, grinned at Mason. "All right, we have our party."

"You're sure it's the one we want?" Mason asked.

"Hell, no!" Tragg said. "The way we work we're not sure of anything. We just run down leads, that's all. We run down a hundred leads and finally get the one we want. Sometimes the one we want is the second one we run down, sometimes it's the one hundredth. Sometimes we run down a hundred leads and don't get anything. This looks pretty live. A woman about thirty years old, height, five-feet-four, weight, 115 to 120, called for a taxi to go to the Ancordia Apartments last night. She gave the name of Miss Harper. We chased down the number of the cab, found that he took her to the Dormain Apartments in Mesa Vista, and that's where we're going now."

"About a chance in a hundred?" Mason asked.

"Make it one in ten," Tragg said. "But I have an idea it'll pay off. Remember the police system is to cover leads. We ring doorbells. We cover a hundred different leads to find the one we want, but we have a hundred people we can put on the job if we have to. And don't ever discount the efficiency of that system, Mason. It pays off. We may look pretty damned stupid when we're running down one of the leads that takes us up a blind alley, but sooner or later we'll get on the right trail."

Tragg piloted the car through the city traffic with a deft sureness that marks the professional driver.

"You're out in traffic a lot," Mason said. "Have any accidents?"

"Hell, no!" Tragg told him. "The taxpayers don't like to have their cars smashed up."

"How do you avoid them?"

"By avoiding them."

"How?"

"You keep alert. You watch the other guy. Accidents are caused by people being discourteous, paying too little attention to what they're doing, and not watching the other guy.

"When I've got a car, I know damn well *I'm* not going to hit somebody. It's the other man who's going to hit me; therefore, the other man is the guy I watch. This is a cinch. But remember that we get leads we have to run down on bad nights, holidays, rush-hour traffic. . . . And the really bad hours are around one to four o'clock in the morning. The man who's had a few drinks and knows he's had a few drinks is pretty apt to be driving cautiously. In fact, the traffic boys pick up a lot of those fellows because they're going too slowly and too cautiously.

"The boy that's really dangerous is the guy who's been whooping it up until two or three o'clock in the morning, and then when he starts home, he's so drunk he doesn't realize he's drunk. About that time he gets a feeling of great superiority and feels that if he can only go through an intersection fast enough, nobody can get halfway across the intersection before he's *all* the way through it. It sounds like swell reasoning when you're drunk, at least that's what they tell me."

Tragg chuckled a few times, drove to Mesa Vista, then drove steadily along one of the main streets, turned to the left, then to the right and slowed his car.

"You know where every apartment house in the county is located?" Mason asked.

"Damned near," Tragg said. "I've been on this job a long time. You'd better come up with me."

Tragg picked up the transmitter, said, "Car XX-Special, out of contact for a short time and parked at the location of the last lead I received on the telephone. Will report in when

I get back in circulation."

The voice on the loud-speaker said, "Car XX-Special, out until report."

"Come on," Tragg said to Mason.

The Dormain Apartments had a rather pretentious front and a swinging door to the lobby. A clerk looked up as Mason and Lt. Tragg entered the lobby, looked down, then suddenly did a double take.

Tragg walked over to the desk. "You have a Harper here?" he asked.

"We have two Harpers. Which one did you want?"

"A woman," Tragg said. "Around thirty; height, five-feet four; weight, maybe 120 pounds."

"That would be Loretta Nann Harper. I'll give her a ring."

Tragg slid a leather folder on the desk, opened it to show a gold, numbered badge. "Police officers," he said. "Don't ring, we'll go on up. What's the number?"

"It's 409. I trust there's nothing —"

"Just want to interview a witness," Tragg said. "Forget about it."

He nodded to Mason and they went to the elevator.

"I repeat," Mason said, "being a police officer has its advantages."

"Yeah," Tragg said. "You ought to follow

me around for a while and then you'd change your tune. Think of when you get on the witness stand and some smart lawyer is walking all over you, asking you how the guy was dressed, what color socks he had on, whether he wore a tiepin, how many buttons on his vest, and every time you say you don't know, the guy sneers at you and says, 'You're a police officer, aren't you? You're on the public payrolls. As an officer you're supposed to have a special aptitude for noticing details, aren't you?' "

Mason grinned. "Well, you *may* have something there."

"May have is right," Tragg said. "The guy just throws questions at you and sneers at you and tosses you insults, and the jurors just sit there and grin, getting a great kick out of seeing some lawyer make a monkey out of a dumb cop."

The elevator, which had been on an upper floor, slid to a stop. Tragg and Mason got in. Tragg pushed the fourth-floor button and they were silent until the cage slid smoothly to a stop.

Tragg oriented himself on the numbers, walked down the corridor, knocked on the door of 409.

There was no answer.

Tragg knocked again.

There was a gentle swishing sound of motion from the other side of the door. The door opened a few inches and was held in position by a chain.

The young woman on the inside bent over slightly so that her body could not be seen, only the eyes, nose and forehead.

"Who is it, please?"

Tragg once more displayed his badge. "Lieutenant Tragg, Homicide," he said. "We'd just like to talk with you a minute."

"I . . . I'm dressing."

"Are you decent?"

"Well, yes."

"Okay, let us in."

She hesitated a moment, then released the catch of the safety chain and opened the door. "I mean . . . that is . . . I'm getting ready to dress to go out. I've just had lunch and —"

"Then you haven't been out yet," Tragg said.

"Not yet."

Mason followed Tragg into the apartment. It consisted of a luxuriously furnished sitting room. Through an open bedroom door, sunlight streaming into the room through a fire escape made a barred pattern on an unmade bed. Another partially opened door gave a glimpse of a bathroom, and there was a powder room on the other side of the sitting room.

A swinging door opened in a kitchen, and the aroma of coffee came to their nostrils.

Tragg said, "Nice place you have here."

"I like it."

"Live here alone?"

"If it's any of your business, yes."

"Lots of room."

"I hate to be cramped."

Tragg said, "We're trying to find a young woman who was at the Ancordia Apartments last night, say around nine-forty-five to ten o'clock. We thought perhaps you could help us."

"What makes you think that?"

"Can you?"

"I don't know."

"Were you there?"

"I . . ."

"Well?" Tragg said as she hesitated.

"Is it particularly important, one way or another?"

"Uh-huh."

"May I ask why?"

Tragg said, "I'd prefer to have you answer my question first, ma'am. Why did you give the name of Beatrice Cornell when George Ansley let you out in front of the apartment house?"

"Does he say I did that?"

"Did you?" Tragg asked.

"Really, Mister — Lieutenant — I'd like to find out why you're asking these questions."

"To get information," Tragg said. "We're investigating a crime. Now, you can answer these questions very simply, and then I'll be in a position to ask you about the automobile accident."

"What accident?"

"The accident where you were pitched out of the car at Meridith Borden's place, the accident where you grabbed the other young woman by the ankles and dragged her away from the car, then slid down onto the ground and started calling for help."

Loretta Harper bit her lip, frowned, said, "Sit down, Lieutenant Tragg. And this is . . . ?"

"Mr. Mason," the lawyer said, bowing.

"I . . . I hope you can keep my name out of this, Lieutenant."

"Well, you'd better tell us about it. How did it happen you were driving a stolen car?"

"*I* was driving a stolen car!" she exclaimed with such vehement emphasis on the *I* that Tragg cocked a quizzical eyebrow.

"Weren't you?" he asked.

"Heavens, no! Dawn Manning was driving the car, and she was driving like a crazy person."

"How did it happen you were with her?"

"She forced me to get into the car."

"How?"

"With a gun."

"That's kidnaping."

"Of course, it is. I was so mad at her I could have killed her."

"Well, go ahead," Tragg said. "What happened?"

"She accused me of playing around with her ex-husband."

"Were you?"

"She had absolutely no right to say the things she did. She and Frank are divorced and she doesn't have any control over him. She certainly doesn't let anyone have any control over her, I can tell you that much. She does exactly as she likes, and —"

"Who's Frank?" Lt. Tragg asked.

"Frank Ferney, her ex-husband."

"And her name?"

"Dawn Manning is her *professional* name."

"What profession?"

"You should ask *me!* You're an officer."

"And how did you happen to get into this stolen car?"

"You're *certain* it was stolen?"

"That's right. A Cadillac, license number CVX 266. It was stolen last night."

"I'll bet she did that so no one could trace her."

"Well, suppose you tell us about it," Tragg said.

"I had a little dinner party last night, a foursome, people who were very intimate friends — a married couple.

"We ran out of cigarettes and ice cubes. I went out to get them and a few other supplies. My friends were watching television.

"It was sometime after eight o'clock, eight-forty-five perhaps. I had stopped to wait for a traffic signal. When the signal changed, I started to walk across, and this car swung right in front of me, blocking the way. It came to a stop. The right-hand door swung open and Dawn Manning said, 'Get in.' "

"You know her?" Tragg asked.

"I've never met her, but I know her by sight."

"She knows you?"

"Apparently."

"What did she say?"

"She said, 'Get in, Loretta, I want to talk with you.' "

"What did you do?"

"I hesitated and she said again, 'I can't stay here all night, I'm blocking traffic. Get in.' "

"Then what happened?"

"There was something in her voice that alarmed me. I started to pull back and then I saw the gun she was pointing at me. She

137

was holding it right on a level with the seat. She said, with deadly earnestness, 'I said get in, and I meant it. You and I are going to have a talk.' "

"So what did you do?"

"I got in. I thought perhaps that would be the best thing to do. I felt certain she was going to shoot if I refused to get in the car."

"Then what?"

"She started to drive like mad. She was half-hysterical, pouring out a whole mess of things."

"Such as what?"

"That Frank — that's Frank Ferney, her ex-husband — had told her over a year ago that he'd gone to Reno and secured a divorce. Dawn said she had acted on the assumption she was free to remarry. Then she'd decided to check up on it, and an attorney had told her no such divorce had ever been granted, that Frank had admitted he'd never gone ahead to finish the divorce and wouldn't do so unless he received a piece of money. He said some rich amateur photographer was giving Dawn a tumble.

"She was so mad about it I thought perhaps she'd shoot Frank and me, too. She said I'd been playing around with Frank and she was going to make us both sign a statement."

"Did she say what would happen otherwise?"

"No, she didn't say, but she had that gun."

"Go on," Tragg said. "Take it from there."

"She was like a crazy woman. I think she was half-hysterical and jealous and upset and frightened. She drove the car like mad and when we came to Borden's place she started to turn in, and, just as she did, saw apparently for the first time a car that was coming out. She slammed on the brakes on wet pavement just as she was making a turn. The tires skidded all over the pavement. We just barely hit the bumper of the other car and crashed through the hedge. I guess we turned completely around. It felt like it to me.

"The car crashed through a hedge and turned over. The doors on the front of the car flew open, or perhaps she opened the door on the driver's side. I know I had opened the door on my side and I was thrown out. I skidded across the grass for a ways and sat up feeling pretty bruised and dazed. And then I saw the glow of a light of some kind and saw this man bending over a figure by the car.

"I had a glimpse in the weak light that was given by the flashlight of Dawn Manning lying there unconscious where she'd been thrown from the car and had skidded on the wet grass."

"Go on," Tragg said. "What happened?"

"Well, then this man seemed to be having trouble with the flashlight. It went out and he threw it into the darkness. I heard it from where I was crouching, dazed and shaken and wondering just what had happened, and whether she still had the gun."

"Go on," Tragg said.

"Well, I . . . I don't feel very proud of this, Lieutenant, but it seemed to be the best thing at the moment and . . . well, at a time like that you just have to think of yourself and for yourself."

"Go on, go on, what did you *do?* Never mind the explanations or the alibis."

"Well, I saw this young man running over toward the driveway to the house and I knew he was going to ask for help and all of that, and I just didn't want to be mixed up in that sort of a mess. In fact, I can't afford to have my name dragged into court or get a lot of newspaper notoriety.

"I grabbed Dawn Manning by the ankles and started pulling. The grass was wet from the rain, and she slid along just as easily as though I had been dragging a big sled. I got her out of the way and put myself in the same position she'd been occupying. I pulled my skirts way up as though I'd skidded. Then I called out for help, and . . . well, this young man came back and I let him get a good look at my legs and then help me up. I got my purse, and in the dark wondered if I could have made a mistake and had Dawn's purse instead of mine. So I stalled around, dove into the car for the second time after my raincoat, found a second purse, concealed it in the folds of the coat and got out.

"I told him that I had been driving the car. I didn't want to have any trouble about it. I let him drive me into the city. I told him it was my car and kidded him along so he didn't ask to see my driving license. I was desperately trying to think of some name I could give him, and then I remembered some-one had told me about a telephone service given by Beatrice Cornell over at the Ancordia Apartments, so I just gave him her name. I knew it would be on the mailbox in case he wanted to check on it, and . . . well, I let him drive me there and let him think he was driving me home.

"He told me his name was Ansley and he was very, very nice. I let him kiss me good night, then I rang the bell of Beatrice Cornell's apartment. She buzzed the lock on the door. I went in, sat in the lobby until Mr. Ansley drove off, then I telephoned for a taxicab and came back here to this apartment."

"Then what?"

"That's all."

"Why did she drive to Meridith Borden's place?"

"That's where her husband works. Frank is associated in some capacity with Meridith Borden. She thought he was there. He wasn't. Actually, he was the fourth guest at my dinner party. He's my boy friend."

"And you left her there in the grounds?" Tragg asked.

"Yes."

"Unconscious?"

"Yes . . . I didn't know what else to do. I had to look out for myself."

Lt. Tragg frowned thoughtfully, fished a cigar from his pocket. "Mind if I smoke?" he asked.

"I'd love it," Loretta Harper said.

The officer regarded her with quizzical appraisal. "Either you," he said, "or this Manning woman is lying. I suppose you know that."

"I can readily imagine it," she said. "Any woman who will take chances on threatening another woman with a gun and pulling a kidnap stunt like that would naturally be expected to lie about it, wouldn't she?"

"And you've got her purse?"

"Yes. I took both purses only because I wanted to be absolutely certain I didn't leave mine behind. I couldn't afford to be mixed up in the thing — and I'll be frank with you, Lieutenant Tragg, Frank and I are . . . well, he's my boy friend."

"I'll want her purse. Did you look in it?"

"Only just to be certain it was hers."

Tragg scraped a match into flame and puffed the end of his cigar into a glowing red circle. "Okay," he said, "let's see it."

She opened a drawer, took out a purse and handed it to Lt. Tragg, who started to open it and look inside, then changed his mind.

Mason said, "I'd like to fix the time element, Miss Harper. Can you tell me exactly when Dawn Manning picked you up?"

"Not the exact minute. I would say it was somewhere between eight-forty and — oh, say a few minutes before nine, right around there sometime."

"And when you had the accident?"

"It must have been nine o'clock or a few minutes after that."

"Then Ansley got out of his car and came running over to where Dawn Manning was lying?"

"That's right."

"And from that point on you were in his company until . . . well, suppose you tell us. Until about what time?"

"I would say I was with him there in the grounds until right around nine-twenty, and

143

then he drove me to the Ancordia Apartments."

"Do you think there's any chance you're mistaken about the time — about any of the times?"

"No. That is, my times are approximate only."

"But you've fixed them as best you can?"

"Yes."

Tragg's eyes narrowed. "You know, Mason," he said, "you're trying to cross-examine this witness. You're getting her story sewed up as much as possible."

"I'm assuming she's telling the truth," Mason said.

"In the event, somebody else isn't."

"I have to make allowances for that also, Lieutenant."

Tragg said to Loretta Harper, "I suppose you know that you violated the Motor Vehicle Act in not reporting an accident where a person was injured."

"I don't think I did," she said. "I wasn't driving the car."

"And," Tragg went on, "since an assault with a deadly weapon was made on you and you didn't report that to the police, you concealed a felony."

"I don't care to prosecute for private reasons. And I don't think the law compels me to go into court and file a complaint on which I wouldn't prosecute."

Tragg twisted the cigar around in his mouth. "Well," he said, "you're going to have to take a ride up to the D.A.'s office and talk things over a bit. Mason, this is where you came in."

Mason grinned. "You mean this is where I go out."

"The same thing," Tragg said.

Mason shook hands with him. "Thanks, Lieutenant."

"Don't mention it," Tragg said. And then added with a grin, "*I'm* sure *I* won't!"

Chapter 8

Mason called Beatrice Cornell's number. "Perry Mason talking," he said when he heard her voice on the line. "How well do you know Dawn Manning?"

"Not too well."

"Would she lie?"

"About what?"

"About a murder."

"You mean if she were involved?"

"That's right."

"Sure, she'd lie," Beatrice Cornell said. "Who wouldn't?"

"How is she otherwise?"

"Nice."

"What do you mean by nice?"

"I mean nice."

"Boy friends?"

"What the hell, she's normal."

"Do you keep records of your calls there?"

"Yes."

"What time was it when someone rang your doorbell and then didn't go on in?"

"I can't tell you that. I don't keep records of things like that, but I think it was about ten."

"Do you remember when I called you and asked you about an automobile accident and you said you hadn't been in one?"

"Of course."

"Would you have a record of the time of that call?"

"Sure," she said. "I record all telephone conversations."

"And the time?"

"And the time," she said. "I have a tape recorder and whenever the phone rings, and before I answer it, I pick up a time clock stamp and stamp that on the piece of paper. Then I mark down the figure which shows on the footage indicator of the tape recorder, switch on the tape recorder and then answer the telephone."

"And what about this particular call that I placed?"

"I simply marked that personal."

"But the conversation would be saved?"

"Yes."

"On the tape recorder?"

"That's right."

"And the time?"

She said, "While I've been talking with you, Mr. Mason, I've been pawing through papers looking for the time sheet. Give me just a minute more and I think I can find it."

Mason grinned. "How about *this* conversation? Is it being recorded?"

"It's being recorded," she said. "I — Here we are. It was ten-twenty-three when you called, Mr. Mason."

"Thanks a lot," Mason told her. "Try and keep that record straight, will you, so you'll know the time?"

"It's all straight," she said, "and this conversation is recorded. I can always refer back to it and tell you the time I gave you."

"That's fine," Mason told her. "Thanks a lot."

He hung up and called his office.

"Hello, Gertie," Mason said when the receptionist and switchboard operator answered the phone. "Della isn't around, is she?"

"No," she said. "You told her to take the day off because she'd been working late last night."

"That's right, I did. She hasn't shown up?"

"No."

"Anyone looking for me?" Mason asked.

"Lots of people."

"Anyone in the office now?"

"Yes."

"Waiting?"

"That's right."

"Anyone who looks official?"

"I don't think so."

"Can you tell me who it is?"

"He says his name is Ansley, George Ansley. You left a message for him."

Mason's voice showed excitement. "Put him in my private office, Gertie," he said. "Lock the door of the private office and don't let anyone in there. Tell him to wait. I'm coming right up."

Leaving his car parked in the parking lot at the Family Kitchen Cafeteria, Mason took a cab direct to his office, went up in the elevator, hurried down the corridor, unlocked the door of his private office and found George Ansley seated in the big, overstuffed chair reading a newspaper.

"Hello, Mr. Mason," Ansley said. "Gosh, I'm glad you showed up. What's new?"

"*You* should ask *me!*" Mason told him.

Ansley raised his eyebrows. "What's the matter?"

"Have you been out of circulation all day?" Mason asked.

"Not all day. I checked in about two o'clock this afternoon and . . . well, I saw the paper."

"That was the first you'd known about it?" Mason asked.

Ansley nodded.

"Now look here," Mason told him, "I want

149

to know *exactly* what happened at your interview with Borden, everything that was said by either party, and I want to know whether you went back to Borden's place after you left me."

Ansley straightened in the chair. "*I* go back to Borden's place?"

Mason nodded.

"Good heavens! You don't mean that anyone would think I could have gone back there, and — ?"

"Why not?" Mason asked. "The building and contract construction inspectors start picking on you. You get the tip to go and see Meridith Borden. Borden is a crooked politician. He's smart enough so he doesn't hold office himself, but acts as go-between.

"It was to Borden's financial advantage to have you come and see him. Surely you aren't so naïve that the possibility hadn't occurred to you that Borden was responsible for all of your troubles — putting you in such a position that you'd have to come to him."

"Of course he was responsible," Ansley said. "That's the way he worked."

"You didn't have a gun, did you?" Mason asked.

"No."

"Where's your car?" Mason asked.

"In the parking lot down here."

"Okay," Mason said, "let's go take a look. Let's look in your glove compartment."

"For what?"

"Evidence."

"Of what?"

"Anything," Mason said. "I'm just checking."

The lawyer opened the door and led the way down the corridor. They descended in the elevator, went to the parking lot, and Ansley pulled out a key container. He fitted the key in the lock of the glove compartment, turned the key, then frowned and said, "Wait a minute, that's the wrong way."

"You're locking it now," Mason said.

"It won't turn the other way."

"Then it probably was unlocked all the time."

Ansley turned the key and said sheepishly, "I guess it was."

Ansley opened the glove compartment. "I usually keep it locked. I must have unlocked it the other night and left it unlocked."

"Let's take a look," Mason said.

"My God!" Ansley exclaimed. "There's a gun in there!"

Ansley reached in to take out the weapon. Mason jerked his arm away.

"Close the glove compartment," Mason said.

"But there's . . . there's a gun there, a blue-steel revolver."

"Close the glove compartment," Mason said.

A voice behind them said, "Mind if I look?"

Mason whirled to see Lt. Tragg standing behind him.

Tragg pushed Mason to one side, showed Ansley a leather container with a gold badge. "Lieutenant Tragg of Homicide," he said.

Lieutenant Tragg reached inside the glove compartment and took out the gun.

"Yours?" he asked Ansley.

"Definitely not. I've never seen it before."

Tragg said, "I guess we'd better sort of take this gun along and check it. You know, Borden was killed with a .38 Colt."

"You don't mean he was killed with *this* gun," Ansley said.

"Oh, sure, sure, not with *your* gun. But just the same, we'd better take it along. The ballistics department will want to play around with it, and then they'll give you a clean bill of health. You won't have anything to worry about. You'll come with me."

"I tell you it isn't *my* gun."

"Oh sure, I know. It just parked itself in your car because it didn't have any place to go. Let's go take a ride and see what Ballistics has to say about the gun."

152

"Mason coming with us?" Ansley asked.

"No," Tragg said, grinning. "Mason has had a busy day and he's been away from his office. He has a lot of stuff to take care of up there. We won't need to bother Mr. Mason. There isn't anything you have on your mind, no reason why you *should* have a lawyer with you, is there?"

"No, certainly not."

"That's what I thought," Tragg said. "Now, if you don't mind, we'll just take this gun and go on up to Headquarters. Probably you'd better drive up in your car. The boys may want to check the car a little bit, find out when you last saw Meridith Borden, and so on. You know how those things are. . . . Okay, Perry, we'll see you later. I'm sorry to have to inconvenience your client, but you know how those things are."

"I certainly do," Mason said dryly, as Tragg took Ansley's arm and virtually pushed him into the automobile.

Chapter 9

The clerk of Judge Erwood's court indicated the spectators could be seated. The judge called the case, "People versus Ansley."

"Ready for the defendant," Mason said.

"Ready for the prosecution," Sam Drew, one of Hamilton Burger's chief trial deputies, said.

"Proceed with the case," Judge Erwood said.

Sam Drew got to his feet. "May the Court please, I think at the start it would be well to have the situation definitely understood. This is a preliminary hearing. The prosecution frankly admits that it doesn't have any intention of putting on enough evidence at this time to convict the defendant of first-degree murder. But it certainly does intend to put on enough evidence to show that first-degree murder has been committed and that there are reasonable grounds to believe the defendant committed that murder.

"As we understand it, that's the sole function of a preliminary hearing."

"That is correct," Judge Erwood said. "This is a preliminary hearing. The Court has noted that some attorneys seem to have an erroneous idea of the issues at a preliminary hearing. We're not trying the defendant now and, above all, we're not trying to find out if the evidence introduced by the prosecution proves him guilty beyond all reasonable doubt.

"All the prosecution is *trying* to do here, and all the prosecution *needs* to try to do here, is to prove that a crime has been committed and that there is reasonable ground to believe the defendant is guilty thereof.

"The Court is going to restrict the issues in this case, and the Court is not going to permit any dramatics. Is that understood, gentlemen?"

"Quite, Your Honor," Mason said, with great cheerfulness.

"Exactly," Sam Drew said.

"Who's your first witness?"

Drew called a surveyor who gave a sketch of the Borden estate and showed its location. He also introduced a map of the city and the suburbs and the location of the Golden Owl Night Club.

"The Court will take judicial cognizance of the location of the various cities in the county," Judge Erwood said.

"Let's not take up the time of the Court with anything except the essential facts. Do you wish to cross-examine this witness, Mr. Mason?"

"No, Your Honor."

"Very well, the witness is excused. Call your next witness," Judge Erwood said.

Drew's next witness was Marianna Fremont, who stated that she had been Meridith Borden's housekeeper for some years. Monday was her day off because quite frequently Meridith Borden did entertaining on Sunday. On Tuesday morning, when she drove up in her car, she had found the gates locked, indicating that Meridith Borden was not up as yet. That was not particularly unusual. The housekeeper had a key, she inserted the key in the electric connection, pressed the button, and the motors rolled the gates back wide open. The housekeeper had driven in and parked her car in its accustomed place in the back yard.

"Then what did you do?" Drew asked.

"Then I went to the house and opened the door and went in."

"Did you see anything unusual?"

"Not at that time, no, sir."

"What did you do?"

"I cooked Mr. Borden's breakfast and then went to his room to call him. Sometimes he

156

would come out for breakfast in a robe, sometimes he had me bring breakfast to him."

"And did you notice anything unusual then?"

"Yes."

"What?"

"There was no sign of him in his bedroom."

"What did you do, if anything?"

"I looked to see if he had left me a note. Sometimes when he was called out overnight he'd leave a note telling me when to expect him."

"Those notes were left in a regular place?"

"Yes."

"Did you find any note that morning?"

"No, sir."

"Very well," Drew said. "Tell us what happened after that."

"Well, I started looking the place over after I found that Mr. Borden hadn't slept in his bed that night."

"Now, just a minute, that's a conclusion," Drew said. "And, while this hearing isn't like a trial before a jury, I think we'd better keep the record in shape. When you said his bed hadn't been slept in, what do you mean?"

"Well, his bed was made fresh."

"Go on."

"Well, then I started looking around and went into the studio."

"Now, what's the studio?"

"That's the room where he did his photography."

"Can you describe it?"

"Well, it's just a room. It's up a short flight of stairs, and it's arranged with a big skylight on the north, a big, long slanting window so he could get the right kind of illumination. There's ground glass in the windows. And then there are a lot of electrical outlets so he could turn floodlights on and use spotlights."

"Mr. Borden used this room?"

"Oh, yes, he used it lots. He was a photographer and liked to photograph things, particularly people."

"And when you went into that room, what did you find?"

"I found Mr. Borden sprawled out on the floor with a bullet hole —"

"Tut-tut. Now, *you* don't *know* it was a bullet hole," Drew interrupted. "You saw something which directed your attention to his chest?"

"Yes. There'd been a lot of bleeding coming from a hole in the chest."

"Mr. Borden was dead?"

"Oh, yes, he was stiff as a board."

"So what did you do?"

"I called the police."

"That's all," Drew said.

"Do you wish to cross-examine?" Judge Erwood asked Mason.

"This photographic studio," Mason said, "can you describe it a little better? Was there anything in it other than what you have mentioned?"

"Oh, yes. A darkroom opens off it. There's a stand with a portrait camera on wheels so you can move it forward and back. And there are a lot of curtains. You know, great big, roller-shade things like curtains that have painted scenery for a background. You know the type of thing photographers use, like beach scenery and mountain scenery and all that."

"Can you tell us just how Mr. Borden was lying?"

"Well, he was on his back with — It's hard to describe. He was all stiff and backward."

"We have a photograph taken by the police photographer," Drew said.

"I'll stipulate it may go in evidence," Mason said, "and that will eliminate the necessity of asking any more questions of this witness."

Drew produced an eight-by-ten photograph, handed one copy to Mason, one copy to Judge Erwood and one copy to the clerk of the court.

"This photograph will be received in evidence," Judge Erwood said. "Call your next witness."

"Officer Gordon C. Gibbs," Drew said.

Gibbs came forward and was sworn.

"You're a police officer connected with the Metropolitan Police Force?"

"Yes, sir."

"On last Tuesday, did you have occasion to enter the apartment leased by the defendant?"

"I did, yes, sir."

"Did you have a search warrant?"

"Yes, sir."

"What were you looking for?"

"Bloody clothing, a murder weapon, anything that would indicate the defendant had been involved in a crime of violence."

"Did you find any of the things you were looking for?"

"Yes, sir."

"What did you find?"

"I found a suit of clothes with rusty brown spots all over them. I took these clothes to the police laboratory and they found the spots were —"

"Just a moment!" Drew snapped out the interruption as Mason was getting to his feet. "The laboratory expert will testify as to what he found. Now did you do anything in the way of identifying this suit of clothes?"

"I did, sir."

"What?"

"I took it to the cleaner whose mark was on the clothes and asked him if he was familiar with the suit and how often he'd seen it and who had sent it in when it had been cleaned. I suppose I can't testify to his answers."

"That's right, you can't," Drew said.

Ansley leaned forward and whispered to Mason, "That was a suit I'd worn when I had one of my nosebleeds. I had them at intervals. This was a windy day, and I had to walk from the job to where I'd parked my car."

Mason turned his attention to the police witness.

"Cross-examine," Drew said.

"You don't know of your own knowledge that these were bloodstains, do you?" Mason asked.

"No, sir."

"You don't know of your own knowledge that it was the defendant's suit?"

"No, sir."

"You don't know of your own knowledge that these stains weren't the result of the defendant's having a bloody nose, do you?"

"No, sir."

"All you know is you found a suit of clothes."

"Yes, sir."

"You tried to check the cleaning marks on that suit of clothes and you delivered it to the police laboratory, is that right?"

"Yes, sir."

"And that's really *all* you know about that suit of clothes?"

"I know the appearance of the stains on it."

"Certainly," Mason said. "You *thought* they were significant stains, otherwise you wouldn't have bothered with it."

"That's right."

"You don't know how long those stains had been on that suit, do you?"

"I know what the cleaner told me as to when he had last cleaned the suit, and —"

"You're an officer," Mason said. "You know you're supposed to testify as to your own knowledge, and not to what someone told you. Now I'll repeat, you don't know how long those stains had been on that suit, do you?"

"No, sir."

"Thank you," Mason said. "That's all."

"I'll call Lieutenant Tragg to the stand," Drew said.

Lt. Tragg came forward, testified as to his name and occupation.

"Do you know the defendant in this case?"

"Yes, sir."

"When did you first meet him?"

"On Tuesday, the ninth."

"Where did you meet him?"

"In a parking lot."

"Who was with you at that time?"

"No one."

"Who was with the defendant at that time?"

"Mr. Perry Mason, who is acting as his attorney."

"Did you have any conversation with the defendant?"

"Yes, sir."

"Can you state the general subject of that conversation? I won't bother you for the exact words at this time."

"We don't want the witness testifying to his conclusions as to the conversation," Mason said.

"I'm not asking for that. I'm only asking if he can remember generally the subject of the conversation."

"Yes, sir."

"What was it?"

"I asked him about a gun in the glove compartment of his car."

"Now, what did you do at that time?"

"I took a gun from the automobile."

"Where was it?"

"In the glove compartment."

"Can you describe that revolver?"

"Yes, sir. It was a Colt .38-caliber revolver of the type known as a police model."

"Did you have occasion to notice the number?"

"I did."

"What was it?"

"613096."

"What did you do with that gun?"

"I turned it over to the ballistics department."

"Now, Lieutenant," Drew said, "you didn't turn it over to a department, you turned it over to some person in that department."

"That's right, to Alexander Redfield."

"He's the police expert on ballistics?"

"Yes, sir."

"Then what happened?"

"I told the defendant I wanted him to go to Headquarters with me."

"Did he make any objection?"

"No, sir."

"He went to Headquarters?"

"Yes, sir."

"And, while he was there, did he make any statement to you?"

"He did, yes, sir."

"What did he say?"

"He made a statement about what he had done the night before, and about the time he had seen Meridith Borden. I asked him if he had any objection to writing down what he had said and giving us a signed account of what had happened. He said he didn't, so I gave him pencil and paper and he wrote out a document."

"Do you have that document with you?"

"I do, yes, sir."

"That was entirely written, dated and signed by the defendant and is in his handwriting?"

"Yes, sir."

"Did anyone tell him what to put in there?"

"No, sir, only to write down what had happened."

"Did anyone offer him any promises, threats or inducements?"

"No, sir."

"Was he subjected to any physical or mental pressure whatever in order to get him to make this statement?"

"No, sir."

"He did it of his own free will and accord?"

"Yes, sir."

"Do you have that statement here with you?"

"Yes, sir."

"If the Court please," Drew said, "I will offer this gun in evidence and also this statement."

"Very well," Judge Erwood said.

"Those are all the questions I have of this witness at this time. I may wish to recall him later," Drew said.

"Quite all right," Mason said. "I know the witness will be available. We waive cross-examination."

"You waive it?" Drew asked incredulously.

"Certainly," Mason said. "I have no questions, none whatever."

"Call your next witness," Judge Erwood said.

Sam Drew said, "Call Harvey Dennison to the stand, please."

Harvey Dennison came forward and was sworn. He testified that he was an owner and proprietor of a general hardware store known as the Valley View Hardware Company, that he had been with the company for a period of more than three years, that he had examined the Colt revolver, Number 613096, that his records showed that this revolver had been purchased from the wholesaler, placed in stock, but that it had not been sold. He said that some three years ago it had been called to his attention that the gun was missing from the showcase, that this theft had turned up in connection with an inventory which was being taken, and the only possible conclusion was that the gun had been stolen, that there had been two occasions at about that time when the store had been entered by someone who had picked the lock on the back door, that certain things had been missing, but the fact that the gun was missing was not discovered until sometime after the burglaries.

"Any cross-examination?" Sam Drew asked of Mason.

"No cross-examination," Mason said.

"Call Alexander Redfield," Drew said.

Redfield came forward, was sworn and qualified himself as a ballistics expert and an expert on firearms and firearm identification.

"I show you a Colt .38 which has previously been introduced in evidence and is marked People's Exhibit 13. This weapon bears the manufacturer's serial number of 613096. Have you seen that weapon before?"

"I have."

"Have you fired a test bullet from it?"

"I have."

"Describe briefly what you mean by a test bullet."

"Each individual barrel has certain defects, irregularities or individualities; little scratches, projections, et cetera, which leave a mark on any bullet which is fired through that gun."

"Are you referring now to the lands and grooves?"

"Oh, no, those are entirely different. Those leave what is known as class characteristics on a bullet. I am referring now to the striations which are known as the individual character-istics of a bullet."

"And by firing a test bullet through a gun, you collect evidence of these defects and ir-regularities?"

"We do. They cause bullet striations, nu-merous tiny scratches which are spaced at ir-regular distances, yet which are always uniform in any bullet fired from any given barrel."

"You mean that it is possible to identify a bullet which has been fired from any particular barrel?"

"That's right, if you have the gun, the fatal bullet and a test bullet."

"And how do you get these so-called test bullets?"

"We fire the gun into a long box in which there are materials such as cotton waste, pieces of paper, cotton, or things of that sort, to re-tard the bullet without defacing it."

"You fired a test bullet through this gun you are now holding?"

"I did."

"And did you subsequently have occasion to compare that bullet with another bullet?"

"I did."

"Where did you get that bullet?"

"From the coroner."

"When?"

"Tuesday afternoon, the ninth."

"And what can you say, with reference to the two bullets?"

"The bullet given me by the coroner agreed in such a large number of details with test bullets fired from this gun that I have no hesitancy in declaring that the so-called fatal bullet was fired from this gun."

"Do you have the bullet which was given you by the coroner?"

"I do."

"And one of the test bullets?"

"I do."

"Will you produce them, please?"

The witness took two small, plastic vials from his pocket, said, "This is the bullet given me by the coroner which, in my photographs, I refer to as the fatal bullet, and the bullet in this container is what I refer to as the test bullet."

"You made photographs showing a comparison of those bullets?"

"I did. I made photographs in which the test bullet was partially superimposed upon the fatal bullet so that it was possible to follow the striations of the bullets as they continued on the overlapping image."

"The striations matched?"

"Yes, sir."

"Do you have those photographs here?"

"I do, yes, sir."

"I will ask that these be received in evidence," Drew said.

"No objection," Mason announced cheerfully.

"Any cross-examination?" Drew asked Mason.

"None, Your Honor. I have the greatest confidence in Mr. Redfield's integrity and ability."

"That's all," Drew said.

The coroner was then called to testify that, under his supervision and direction, an autopsy had been performed upon the body of Meridith Borden, that a bullet had been found imbedded in the torso of Borden, that this bullet had been carefully removed by the autopsy surgeon, placed in a plastic vial with a screw top, sealed in the vial, and the vial had been turned over by him to Alexander Redfield, the ballistics expert.

"That's all," Drew said.

"No questions on cross-examination," Mason announced.

Judge Erwood settled back in his chair with something akin to relief. Sam Drew, on the other hand, acted like a man who is walking over a mined area and momentarily expects an explosion to blow him into kingdom come. His case was proceeding all too regularly, all too swiftly and according to blueprint specifications. Everyone who was familiar with Perry Mason's courtroom strategy knew he never permitted cases to proceed in such a manner — not for long.

Drew called the autopsy surgeon to the stand and questioned him concerning the findings at the autopsy. The surgeon read from notes stating that he had recovered a .38-caliber bullet which he had placed in a plastic container and turned over to the coroner, who, in his presence, had turned it over to Alexander Redfield; that the bullet which the coroner turned over to Redfield was the same bullet which he had recovered from the body of Meridith Borden, that the bullet had entered the left chest at a point slightly to the left of the median line and had ranged slightly downward, that he had recovered the bullet in the skin of the back, that the bullet had torn one corner of the heart completely out, and that in his opinion, death had been due to this bullet wound and had been virtually instantaneous.

"In addition to your other qualifications," Drew asked, "have you had experience in blood classifications and serology?"

"Yes, sir."

"I show you a suit of clothes on which there are certain spots, and ask you if you have examined those spots."

"I have, yes, sir."

"What are they?"

"Blood."

"Can you tell what kind of blood?"

"Yes, sir."

"What kind?"

"Human blood."

"Can you further classify this human blood as to type?"

"Not on all of the spots. Some of them are too minute to permit a classification. But I have been able to classify the larger spots."

"What classifications?"

"The group that is known as AB."

"Is this the relatively common group?"

"No, sir. It is a very rare blood grouping."

"Can you estimate the percentage of people who have this grouping?"

"I would say not to exceed twelve per cent."

"What type was the blood of the decedent, Meridith Borden?"

"The same type as the blood which appears on this suit, type AB."

"Cross-examine," Drew said.

"Could you tell how old those stains were?" Mason asked.

"Not exactly."

"They had dried and changed color?"

"That is right."

"What is the type of the defendant's blood?" Mason asked.

"I don't know."

"You don't?"

"No. Probably it is type O. That is the most common type. Around fifty per cent of the people have that type."

"But for all you know the defendant's blood may be type AB?"

"That is right. Once we show his suit is spotted with human blood, it's up to him to show that it's his — at least that's the way I look at it."

"That's all," Mason said.

He turned to Ansley and whispered, "What's your blood type?"

"I don't know," Ansley said. "I only know that I was wearing that suit when I had the nosebleed."

"No further questions on cross-examination," Mason said as the witness remained on the witness stand.

"That's all," the Judge said. "Call your next witness, Mr. Prosecutor."

"Call Beeman Nelson," Drew said.

Nelson was sworn, gave his occupation as operator of a cleaning establishment, identified the cleaning mark on the bloodstained suit, stated that he had cleaned and pressed the suit on at least five different occasions, that the suit on each occasion had been received from and delivered to George Ansley, the defendant; that the last date he had cleaned, pressed and delivered the suit to Ansley was about ten days before the murder. At that time the suit had been in good condition and there were no blood spots on it.

"Any questions?" Drew asked Perry Mason.

"None whatever," Mason said.

Judge Erwood indicated impatience, glancing at the clock, quite evidently prepared to make an order binding the defendant over to the higher court for trial.

Drew, noticing the signs of judicial impatience, said, "If the Court please, I have just one or two more witnesses. I feel that I can conclude this case within a short time."

"Go ahead," Judge Erwood said. "Call your witnesses."

"Call Jasper Horn," Drew said.

Jasper Horn, a tall, raw-boned, slow-moving individual, came forward, held up a big, calloused hand and was sworn.

"Your name is Jasper Horn?"

"Yes, sir."

"What's your occupation, Mr. Horn?"

"I'm a foreman."

"Are you acquainted with the defendant, George Ansley?"

"I am, yes, sir."

"Do you work for him, or have you worked for him?"

"That's right. I'm foreman on a job he's doing, building a school out in the west side."

"I'm going to direct your attention to last Monday morning and ask you if you had any conversation with George Ansley."

"Sure, I had lots of conversations with him. He was out on the job and we were looking around."

"Was there anything particularly unusual or annoying — I'll withdraw that. Let me ask you this. Had there been any complaints about the buildings not being up to specifications?"

"Lots of them."

"Was there any particular matter which you were discussing with Mr. Ansley last Monday morning about the problems of inspection?"

"Yes, sir."

"What was it?"

"Well, some of the steel supports in one of the walls had warped a little bit out of line. The distance between centers was not quite uniform, and one or two of them were slightly off."

"Had you previously had some conversation with the inspector about that?"

"I had."

"And what did the inspector tell you?"

"He told me that stuff would have to be

175

fixed up or the wall would have to come out."

"You argued with him?"

"I'll say I argued with him."

"And then, later on, you reported this conversation to Ansley?"

"Sure. I told him about it."

"And did you make a suggestion to Ansley at that time?"

"Yes, sir."

"What was it?"

"I told him that if he was smart, he'd go and see Meridith Borden and his troubles would be over."

"And what did Mr. Ansley say at that time?"

"He told me that he'd take a gun and shoot Borden through the heart before he'd knuckle under to a guy like that and pay tribute. He said that if Borden was making all these troubles for him hoping he'd get a shakedown, Borden was out of luck. He said killing was too good for people like that."

There was a slight murmur in the courtroom.

"Your witness," Drew said.

Mason straightened in his chair. "That conversation was Monday?"

"Yes, sir."

"Had you had previous conversations about defective construction with inspectors?"

"I'll say I had. . . . Nothing else but, if you ask me."

"The inspectors had been rather critical?"

"Mr. Mason," the witness said vehemently, "the inspectors had been tough, mighty tough. They'd crawled all over the job looking for the most microscopic details they could dig up. They'd throw those things at us, make us tear stuff out and replace it. They were crawling all over the place, getting in my hair, hampering construction, driving us all nuts."

"Up until Monday of last week?"

"That's right."

"Including Monday?"

"Including Monday."

"Now, directing your attention to Tuesday morning, did you have any conversation with the inspectors?"

"Just a minute," Sam Drew said, "that's incompetent, irrelevant, immaterial and not proper cross-examination. I didn't ask the witness anything about Tuesday morning."

"I think I'm entitled to examine the witness as to all of his conversations with the inspectors," Mason said. "After all, he's testifying as to conclusions. He's testifying that the inspectors were unreasonable, that they were tough, and so I've got a right to show *all* of the experiences this man has had with inspectors, what he means by saying they were un-

177

reasonable, what he means by saying they were tough. There must be some standard of normal that he is referring to in his own mind."

"I think I'll allow the question," Judge Erwood said.

"Tuesday morning," the witness said, "there was a great big difference. The inspector on the job came to me and told me he was satisfied there had been a substantial compliance with the specifications on the steelwork on the wall. He said he'd watched our work, that he felt it was very good and that he was satisfied we were doing a good job. He said that from now on he was going to leave me pretty much on my own to complete it."

"That was Tuesday morning?" Mason asked.

"Yes, sir."

"Thank you," Mason said. "That's all."

"No further questions," Drew said.

"You're excused," Judge Erwood told the witness.

"I'm going to call Frank Ferney," Drew said.

Ferney came forward and was sworn. "You were in the employ of Meridith Borden in his lifetime?"

"Yes, sir."

"In what capacity?"

"Oh, sort of a general assistant. I did whatever needed to be done."

"You took messages for him?"

"That's right."

"Ran errands?"

"That's right. I did anything and everything that was required. I helped him when he'd entertain, I kept liquor glasses full, tried to keep the guests happy. I did anything that needed to be done."

"Directing your attention to last Monday. Do you have a day off?"

"No, sir. I don't work that way. I'm around most of the time but when I wanted to take off, I just told him I was going."

"And what about last Monday night?"

"I told him I wouldn't be there Monday evening until late. I said I wanted to have an evening with my girl friend."

"And what time did you actually leave last Monday evening?"

"Six o'clock?"

"Are you acquainted with Marianna Fremont, the housekeeper?"

"Certainly."

"Does she do the cooking?"

"When she's there she cooks the meals."

"Mondays are her days off?"

"That's right."

"Who cooks on Mondays?"

"Well, she did the cooking when we didn't have company. Usually he had another cook come in when we were entertaining, or sometimes a caterer brought in a meal if he was entertaining quite a few people.

"When Mr. Borden and I were there alone, I'd scramble up some eggs and cook some bacon for breakfast. We'd usually have a salad for lunch, and sometimes I'd cook up some stuff Monday night. We sort of camped out on the cook's day off unless we were entertaining. If we were, he'd get a caterer or another cook."

"Was any meal cooked last Monday night?"

"He told me he was going to open up some canned sauerkraut and have some weenies. I was going out for dinner."

"What time did he usually eat on Monday evening, if you know?"

"I object, if the Court please," Mason said. "If the testimony has any bearing, it is incumbent to show what actually happened on this particular night. I object to this specific question as being incompetent, irrelevant and immaterial."

Drew said, "It is very important, if the Court please, to get this point established because, while the time of death can only be fixed as between eight-thirty and eleven-thirty from the temperature of the body, the development of the *rigor mortis* and postmortem lividity, the time could be fixed much more accurately if we knew when the last meal was ingested."

Judge Erwood turned to Ferney. "And that is something that you don't know — except by referring to general custom?"

"That's right, Your Honor. Monday night he had the house to himself. He could have gone out there at five minutes after six, after I left, and eaten, or he could have waited until eight-thirty and eaten, or he could have waited until after Ansley had finished with his appointment. I know when we usually ate on Monday night. That's the only way I can fix the time."

"I see," Judge Erwood said thoughtfully. "I think I'll sustain the defendant's objection — as the evidence now stands."

"I think that covers all our questions. You may cross-examine," Drew said to Perry Mason.

"There is a wall surrounding the entire estate?" Mason asked.

"That's right."

"And electric gates?"

"That's right. They're controlled by electricity."

"Is there any other means of ingress and

egress except through those gates?"

"There's a back entrance."

"And where is that?"

"That's in back of the garage."

"Of what does it consist?"

"It's a heavy, solid iron gate which is kept locked at all times."

"You have a key to it?"

"Of course."

"The housekeeper has a key to it."

"Yes, sir."

"And, of course, Mr. Borden had a key to it?"

"Right."

"Are there any other keys?"

"Not that I know of."

"Is that gate wide enough for an automobile to enter?"

"No, sir, just wide enough for a person to go through. It's a heavy, solid iron door. All the traffic comes in through the main gates. There's a rubber tube imbedded in the ground under a movable apron there at the gate, and whenever a car drives in, it rings a bell in the house so that Mr. Borden knows someone's coming in."

"I see," Mason said thoughtfully. "How did the gates close?"

"You could close them by pressing a button in the house, or the gates closed automatically with a timing device which was set for eleven o'clock, although that time could be changed."

"How did the gates open?"

"They had to be opened by pressing a button in the house, or by manipulating a locked switch out on the driveway. If you used the switch in the driveway, the gates would open long enough for a car to go through, and then they'd automatically close again."

"Was there some way of opening the gates from the outside?"

"Sure. There's a switch with a key. You use the key to unlock the switch, press the button and the gates open long enough for a car to drive through, then they automatically close again."

"You had keys to all those switches?"

"Sure."

"And the housekeeper?"

"That's right. She had keys, too."

"There's a telephone there at the gate?"

"That's right."

"And with what is that telephone connected?"

"That's a private line that goes right through to the house where there are two telephones that ring whenever the button is pressed."

"Where are those telephones located?"

"One of them is in Mr. Borden's study, the

other is in the place where I stay, my room."

"And where is your room?"

"Down in the basement."

"Why the two telephones?"

"Because when the gate bell rings, I pick up the receiver and ask who is there and all about it. Mr. Borden would be listening in on his extension. If it was someone Borden wanted to see, he'd then cut in and say, 'This is Mr. Borden himself. I'll open the gates for you and you can drive in.' But if after a while I didn't hear Borden saying anything like that, I'd just tell the guy that I was sorry, the gates were closed for the night, that Borden couldn't be disturbed, and hang up."

"The telephone at the gate connected then with just those two instruments?"

"That's right."

"Mr. Borden spent most of his time in this study?"

"Practically all of it."

"What about the photographic studio?"

"He was up there some of the time, mostly at night."

"Did you ever help him in there?"

"Not him. When he went to the studio, he was to be left alone. You didn't disturb him in that studio."

"He kept the door locked?"

"It had a spring lock on it."

"Sometimes he worked with models?"

Drew said, "If the Court please, this is not proper cross-examination. It calls for matters which are entirely extraneous, and unquestionably represents simply a fishing expedition on the part of counsel."

"The Court is inclined to agree with that statement," Judge Erwood said. "The objection is sustained."

"That's all," Mason said.

"No further questions," Drew said.

Drew looked at the clock. "If the Court please, it is approaching the hour of the noon adjournment. I feel that we have presented this case expeditiously. That is our entire case. We feel we have proved the elements necessary to bind the defendant over."

Judge Erwood said, "I think you have more than established them. You could have quit half an hour ago and still have been entitled to an order binding the defendant over. It is, therefore, the order of this Court that the defendant be bound over to —"

"May the Court please," Mason said, getting to his feet.

Judge Erwood frowned his annoyance. "Yes, what is it, Counselor?"

Mason said, "The defense has the right to put on testimony."

"Certainly," Judge Erwood said. "I am not

trying to foreclose you from putting on a defense, if you desire, although I may state that in hearings of this sort it is rather unusual for the defense to put on a case. Very frankly, Mr. Mason, since there is no jury present, I feel free to state that I don't know what defense you could possibly put on which would keep the Court from binding the defendant over. You might or might not have something that would raise a reasonable doubt in the mind of a jury, but as far as this Court is concerned, the evidence is simply overwhelming that a murder was committed and that there is probable cause to believe that the defendant committed the crime."

"Except for one thing, if the Court please," Mason said. "There is one point which is very much in doubt."

"I don't see it," Judge Erwood said somewhat testily.

"The time element," Mason said. "If my client committed the murder, he must have done so before nine o'clock."

"The evidence doesn't so show."

"Well, the evidence can be made to so show," Mason said, "and we propose to show that Meridith Borden was alive and well a long time after nine o'clock."

Judge Erwood stroked his chin. "Well," he said at length, "that, of course, would be a perfect defense *if* you could establish it, Mr. Mason."

"We propose to establish it."

"How long will you take?"

"At least all afternoon," Mason said.

Judge Erwood said, "I have rather a full calendar and I had anticipated this was a routine matter that would perhaps consume an hour, certainly not more than the entire morning."

"I am sorry, Your Honor, I'm quite certain that I didn't give the Court any impression that such would be the case."

"No, *you* didn't," Judge Erwood admitted. "I guess perhaps it was due somewhat to a misunderstanding. These matters usually are disposed of rather promptly. However, I have no desire to foreclose the defendant from putting on a case. I will state this, Mr. Mason, proof of an alibi will have to be very, very clear and very, very convincing in order to keep the Court from binding the defendant over.

"You are a veteran trial attorney and are, of course, aware of the disadvantages to a defendant of putting on a defense at a preliminary examination. Now then, in the face of that statement of the Court, do you wish to proceed?"

"I do."

"Very well," Judge Erwood said. "I will make one more statement, which is that I have noticed in the press that in certain cases where you have appeared in a preliminary examination there have been dramatic developments, developments which in my opinion have not been justified.

"I mean no personal criticism by this. It is simply my opinion that Courts have been far too lenient with counsel in permitting a certain type of evidence to be brought into the preliminary hearing. I do not intend to foreclose any of the rights of the defendant, but, on the other hand, I certainly do not intend to open the door to a lot of extraneous matter."

"Very well, Your Honor," Mason said. "I wish to address my proof to the Court on the theory that if the defendant killed Meridith Borden, the crime must have been committed before nine o'clock in the evening. I think I can show conclusively that the crime was *not* committed prior to nine o'clock."

"Very well," Judge Erwood said. "The Court will take a recess and —"

"Just a moment. If I may have the indulgence of the Court," Mason interrupted, "I dislike to interrupt, but there is one matter that may be of great importance to the defendant."

"What is that?"

"The body of Meridith Borden was found in the photographic studio. The inference would therefore be that after his interview with the defendant, Borden went to his photographic studio to take photographs, and that therefore someone must have been with him. Borden would hardly be taking photographs of himself."

Judge Erwood frowned. "That reasoning, Mr. Mason, is predicated entirely upon your belief in whatever story the defendant may have told you. If you propose to base your alibi on evidence of this kind, you are wasting your time.

"For all the Court knows, Meridith Borden could have been talking with the defendant, George Ansley, in the photographic studio. Borden might have been taking George Ansley's picture.

"I am assuming that the defendant is prepared to testify that his interview took place in the study, but this Court would pay absolutely no attention to such testimony. A jury might or might not believe the defendant. As far as this Court is concerned, on a preliminary examination where it appears that a murder has been committed with the murder weapon found in the defendant's possession, the Court is certainly not going to take the defendant's unsupported word as proof that he was not in the room where the murder was committed."

"I understand that, Your Honor," Mason said, "and I am not asking the Court to take his word. I would, however, like to ask the deputy district attorney if it isn't true that there was evidence in the studio that certain photographs had been taken that evening. If so, I wish to have those photographs produced in evidence."

Drew said testily, "We don't have to disclose all our evidence to the defense."

"But were there no exposed plates?" Mason asked. "Nothing, perhaps, in the camera?"

"There were exposed plates," Drew said, "and there was an exposed plate in the camera; but there is no indication as to *when* the plate was exposed."

"If the Court please," Mason said, "I feel that some of this can be connected up. If those exposed films have not been developed, I feel that they should be developed so that we can see what is on them."

"Have those films been developed?" Judge Erwood asked Sam Drew.

"They have, Your Honor."

"I take it," Judge Erwood said, "that if there were photographs of the defendant, those films or prints made from those films would have been introduced in evidence."

190

"That is quite correct," Drew said testily. "The decedent, at the time of his death, was carrying on a camera contest with some of his cronies. They were having a somewhat good-natured contest to see who could get the best calendar-girl photograph. It is our opinion that the films which were in the camera had been photographed either during the day or during the preceding day. We don't feel that there was any significance attached to Mr. Borden's presence in the photographic studio, except that he probably went there to get these films out of the camera and develop the exposed films which he had. He probably was rather anxious to get started on his work in this contest."

Mason said, "I'd like to suggest to the prosecution that those films be brought into court this afternoon, or at least prints from those films."

"I see no reason for that whatever," Drew said. "This is not a trial before a jury. The prosecution doesn't need to disclose any more than enough evidence to show that a crime has been committed and that there is reasonable ground to believe that the defendant committed that crime."

"That's right," Judge Erwood said. "But where the defense wishes to put on testimony, it *does* have the right to subpoena witnesses.

191

The defense could subpoena the persons who have these films. I think you had better produce them, Mr. Drew, it will save time."

"But they have no bearing on the case, no bearing whatever," Drew said.

"Then you can object to their introduction in evidence. But the defendant, in a preliminary hearing, certainly has the right to subpoena witnesses on his own behalf and to introduce evidence on his own behalf."

Drew yielded with poor grace. "Very well," he said, "I'll bring the pictures into court."

Judge Erwood said, "Court will take a recess until two o'clock this afternoon."

Mason hurried over to Paul Drake. "All right, Paul," he said, "give the signal. Have your men serve subpoenas on Loretta Harper, Dawn Manning, Beatrice Cornell and Frank Ferney."

Drake turned, signaled to one of his men who was in the courtroom by holding up his hand with the thumb down and four fingers extended.

"Okay," he said to Mason. "That's all taken care of, Perry, but I don't see what you're going to do except tip your hand. This judge is going to bind Ansley over, come hell or high water."

"He isn't going to bind him over until I've found out a lot more about the prosecution's case," Mason said. "I'm going to get just as much evidence before the Court as I can."

192

"But," Drake protested, "they'll object on the ground that it's immaterial, and the judge will sustain them."

"Not after I get done, he won't," Mason said. "Either Loretta Harper or Dawn Manning is lying, one or the other. Dawn Manning makes a beautiful picture of sweet innocence, but the cold logic of the situation points to the fact that she probably was turned loose in the grounds at about nine o'clock, and there's no real proof that she didn't go to the house and remain there until after the murder was committed."

"Go to it," Drake said, "I will say it won't do you any good. Sam Drew is one of the happiest men in the whole legal profession right now. He's been able to put on a *prima facie* case, the judge is with him, and he feels you don't stand a ghost of a chance of changing the judge's mind."

Mason grinned. "The presiding judge assigned Judge Erwood to sit on this hearing with the understanding that he would see the case was handled according to the usual cut-and-dried routine. Burger protested I'd been given too much leeway in the past."

"Think you can beat a situation like that?" Drake asked dubiously.

Mason pursed his lips thoughtfully. "I can sure as hell try."

Chapter 10

When court reconvened at two o'clock, Paul Drake had a whispered word of warning for Perry Mason.

"Watch Sam Drew," he said. "He's so tickled he can hardly contain himself. Something has happened during the recess that has given him a big kick. The gossip is that he's passed the word down the line, and Hamilton Burger, the district attorney, is coming in to watch you fall flat on your face."

"Any idea what it's all about?" Mason asked.

"I can't find out," Drake said, "but the whole camp is just bursting with suppressed excitement, and —"

He broke off as Judge Erwood entered the courtroom from his chambers. Everybody stood and waited for the stroke of the gavel which signaled they were to be seated.

"People versus Ansley," Judge Erwood said. "Are you ready to proceed, Mr. Mason?"

"Yes, Your Honor."

"Very well, Mr. Mason, proceed with your case."

Mason said, "As my first witness I will call my secretary, Miss Della Street, to the stand."

Judge Erwood frowned, started to say something, then changed his mind.

Della Street went to the stand, held up her right hand and was sworn.

At that moment the courtroom door opened, and Hamilton Burger, the district attorney, made a personal appearance, quite obviously enjoying the whispered comments as he came lumbering down the aisle, pushed his way through the swinging mahogany gate in the bar and seated himself beside Drew.

Burger made no attempt to conceal the broad grin on his face.

Mason felt his way cautiously through the examination.

"Your name is Della Street and you are now and for some time have been in my employ as my confidential secretary?"

"Yes, sir."

"You are acquainted with the defendant?"

"Yes, sir."

"When did you first see the defendant?"

"On the evening of Monday, the eighth."

"Where did you see him?"

"At the Golden Owl Night Club."

"What was the time?"

"The time was approximately two or three minutes past ten o'clock."

"And what happened?"

"Mr. Ansley approached the table where we were sitting and asked you to —"

Drew held up his hand.

"We object to anything the defendant may have said at that time, as a self-serving declaration, as hearsay and as incompetent, irrelevant and immaterial," Drew said.

"There is no need for the objection," Mason said. "I don't want the witness to relate the conversation. I will just ask you, Miss Street, as to what was done."

"Well, the defendant asked you to do certain things, and after some conversation we left the Golden Owl Night Club."

"At what time?"

"At exactly ten-thirty-two."

"Now, when you say 'we,' who do you mean?"

"You, Mr. Ansley and myself."

"And where did we go?"

"We went to Meridith Borden's place."

"Were the gates open or closed?"

"The gates were open."

"What did we do?"

"We parked the car just outside the gates."

"Then what?"

"We looked around for some ten or fifteen

minutes, I would judge."

"And then what happened?"

"Then a gong sounded and the gates closed."

"Then what happened?"

"Then Mr. Ansley went to the gates, tried to open them and apparently set off a burglar alarm. . . ."

"Objected to as a conclusion of the witness. Move to strike," Drew said.

"Stipulated it may go out," Mason said. "Just what happened?"

"A bell sounded, floodlights came on, on the grounds, and we could hear the barking of dogs."

"Then what?"

"Then we climbed over the wall and a dog came charging at us. Just as you got up on the wall, the dog was snapping at your heels and leaping up at the wall."

"Then what?"

"Then we descended the wall on the other side."

"Do you know what time it was then?"

"It was just after eleven."

"Then what happened?"

"We went to the front gate."

"And what happened there?"

"You looked around and discovered a telephone."

"And what happened?"

"You talked into the telephone."

"Now, just a moment, just a moment," Drew objected. "This is incompetent, irrelevant and immaterial. It is a conclusion of the witness."

"It's no conclusion of the witness," Mason said. "It would be a conclusion if I asked her to whom I was talking, but she is testifying only to a physical fact, that I talked into the telephone. I talked into the telephone and she can testify to that fact."

"Go ahead," Judge Erwood said to Della Street. "The objection is overruled. Any motion to strike is denied. Don't tell us what Mr. Mason said or to whom he talked, just what happened."

"Yes, Your Honor. Then Mr. Mason hung up, and — Would I be permitted to state what he told me?"

Judge Erwood shook his head and said, "Not if the prosecution objects."

"We object," Drew said.

"Very well. That would be hearsay, just go ahead and state what was done if it is at all pertinent."

"I think it is quite pertinent," Mason said. "We are now coming to the part that I feel is very important."

"Very well," Judge Erwood said. "What

happened, Miss Street?"

"Then, after Mr. Mason hung up the telephone, I picked up the telephone and kept pressing the button at regular intervals."

"And what happened?"

"Mr. Borden answered the phone."

"Just a minute, just a minute," Drew said. "We move to strike that out as the conclusion of the witness. No proper foundation laid."

Judge Erwood turned to Della Street, his face showing considerable interest. "You state that Mr. Borden answered?"

"Yes, sir."

"Did you know him in his lifetime?"

"No, Your Honor."

"Then how did you know it was Mr. Borden?"

"He said it was Mr. Borden."

"In other words, there was a voice over the telephone announcing that it was Mr. Borden talking?"

"Yes, Your Honor."

Judge Erwood shook his head. "The objection is sustained. The motion to strike is granted. That is a conclusion of the witness. You may, however, state as nearly as you can recall the conversation which took place over the telephone."

"We object to it, if the Court please," Drew said, "with all due respect to the Court's question. Unless it can be shown definitely that it was Meridith Borden on the other end of the line, we object."

Judge Erwood shook his head. "Counsel has already laid the foundation by showing that the telephone at the gate is connected directly with the house. Now then, Miss Street has testified she pressed the button on the telephone and she had a conversation with someone. She is entitled to relate that conversation. Then it can be shown that the person at the other end of the line was Mr. Borden, either by direct or by circumstantial evidence. The Court may state that the foundation as far as circumstantial evidence is concerned, is pretty well laid at this moment. It appears that Mr. Borden was alone in the house, according to the prosecution's own testimony. According to the testimony of this witness, some man answered the telephone. I have stricken out the statement that the man said he was Mr. Borden, as a means of proving the identity of the person at the other end of the line, but I will permit the witness to state what the conversation was."

Della Street said, "I believe the man's voice asked who was calling. I said that we were passers-by, that we wanted to speak with Mr. Borden. The voice said that it was Mr. Borden speaking, that he didn't want to be disturbed, and I told him that this was a matter of an emergency, that we had reason to believe there was a young woman who had been in an auto accident and who might be wandering around the grounds somewhere.

"Then the man's voice stated that someone had been tampering with the gates; that this had triggered a burglar alarm and released watchdogs; that he would turn off the lights and call the dogs back to the kennels; that the dogs were not going to hurt anyone; that they were trained to hold a person motionless and bark until someone could arrive; that they weren't going to kill anyone. Then the voice asked me who I was, and I refused to give my name, saying I was merely a passer-by."

"Then what?" Mason asked.

"I hung up the telephone and I told you — That is," Della Street amended with a smile at the prosecution's table, "I know I'm not permitted to state what I told you."

"Now, what time was this?" Mason asked.

"It was possibly ten minutes after eleven, perhaps fifteen minutes after eleven, when I had this conversation."

"Then what did we do?"

"We drove Mr. Ansley back to the Golden Owl Night Club where he picked up his car."

"We were with Mr. Ansley until what time?"

"Until right around eleven-thirty, perhaps eleven-thirty-five."

"And we left him where?"

"At the Golden Owl Night Club."

"Then you, yourself and of your own knowledge, can vouch for the whereabouts of the defendant in this case from a time which you estimate to be two or three minutes after ten until eleven-thirty on the evening of the murder?"

"That is right," Della Street said.

Mason turned to Drew.

"You may cross-examine," he said.

Drew, grinning broadly, said, "We have no questions of this witness."

"No cross-examination?" Judge Erwood asked in surprise.

Drew shook his head.

"The Court may point out to you, Mr. Drew, that unless the testimony of this witness is questioned in some way, there is a very strong presumption that she was actually talking with Mr. Borden."

"We understand, Your Honor," Drew said. "But we don't intend to try to establish our rebuttal by cross-examination."

"Very well," Judge Erwood snapped.

"That's all," Mason said. "That's our case, Your Honor."

Judge Erwood looked at the table where

Hamilton Burger and Sam Drew were engaged in smiling conversation. "It would seem, Mr. Prosecutor," the judge said, "that we now have a very material difference in the situation. We have the testimony of a disinterested witness, one whose integrity impresses the Court, that some male person was in the Borden house a few minutes after eleven o'clock, that this male person answered a telephone, that according to the testimony of the prosecution's own witnesses, the only person left in the Borden house at that time was Meridith Borden."

"If the Court please," Hamilton Burger said, smiling indulgently, "we would like to put on some rebuttal evidence before the Court, which will clarify the situation."

"Very well, go ahead, call your witness."

"We recall Frank Ferney," Hamilton Burger said.

Frank Ferney returned to the witness stand.

"You've already been sworn," Hamilton Burger said. "There's no need for you to be sworn again. Have you heard the testimony of Miss Street who was just on the stand?"

"Yes, sir."

"Do you know anything about the conversation that she has related?"

"Yes, sir."

"What do you know about it?"

"I was the person at the other end of the line."

Hamilton Burger grinned triumphantly. "You were the person who said you were Meridith Borden?"

"Yes, sir."

Hamilton Burger bowed with exaggerated courtesy to Perry Mason. "You may cross-examine," he said, and sat down.

Mason arose to face the witness. "You told us," he said, "that you left the Borden house at six o'clock; that you took a night out and had dinner with your girl friend."

"That's right. But I came back. I have my living quarters and I sleep there."

"What time did you get back?"

"Actually it was about — oh, I would say around ten minutes to eleven."

"And how did you get there?" Mason asked.

The witness grinned. Hamilton Burger grinned. Sam Drew grinned.

"I drove back in an automobile," he said.

"Alone?" Mason asked sharply.

"No, sir."

"Who was with you?"

"A woman."

"Who was this woman?"

"Dr. Margaret Callison."

"And who is Dr. Callison?"

"A veterinary."

"How did you enter the premises?"

"We drove up to the locked back gate. Dr. Callison parked her car, and I took a dog out of her car. The dog was on leash. I opened the door, took the dog to the kennel, unlocked the kennel door and put the dog inside. That was at approximately ten minutes to eleven, perhaps five minutes to eleven, by the time I got the dog in there.

"I then asked Dr. Callison if she wanted a drink, and she said she'd run in and have a drink. She wanted to see Mr. Borden and tell him something about the dog."

"So what did you do?"

"I escorted her to the back door of the house, opened the door with my key and we went in."

"Then what?"

"I went to Mr. Borden's study and he wasn't there. I assumed that . . . well, I guess I'm not permitted to say what I assume."

"Go right ahead," Mason said. "I don't hear any objection from the prosecution and I certainly have none. I want to know *exactly* what happened. I'm not afraid of the facts in this case."

"Well, I assumed that he was up in the studio doing some photographic work, perhaps some development, and I suggested to Dr. Callison that we wait a few minutes and see if he came down. I poured a couple of drinks, and about that time the burglar alarm sounded, the lights came on and the kennel doors opened automatically.

"I heard the dogs run to the wall and bark, and then I could tell by the way one of the dogs was barking and jumping that whoever had set off the burglar alarm had gone over the wall. I returned to Dr. Callison and suggested we finish our drinks in a hurry and go see what had happened and what had turned on the burglar alarm.

"Then I went out and whistled the dogs back to the kennel.

"While I was still outside, I heard the telephone ring. I hurried back and found that Dr. Callison had answered the telephone. She told me that some man had asked for Mr. Borden, and she had told him Mr. Borden didn't want to be disturbed."

"Then what?" Mason asked.

"Then, after a short time, the phone continued for a long series of jangling rings."

"So what happened?" Mason asked.

"I answered the telephone. I thought probably it was the police calling about the burglar alarm."

"And what happened?" Mason asked.

"A young woman was on the other end of the telephone. I recognize her voice now as that of Miss Street. She has given a very accurate statement of the conversation which took place over the telephone. That is, I said I was Borden and told her the dogs wouldn't hurt anyone; that I would turn off the light and put the dogs back in the kennels. Actually, I had already put the dogs back."

Mason regarded the witness with thoughtful eyes.

Over at the prosecution table, Hamilton Burger and Sam Drew were grinning expansively at the spectacle of Mason bringing out the prosecution's case on cross-examination. Having resorted to the time-honored trick of asking Ferney only a few devastating questions on direct examination and then terminating their questioning with no explanation, they had virtually forced Mason to crucify himself.

"Is it your custom to state over the telephone that you are Meridith Borden?" Mason asked.

"Sure," the witness said. "At times, when Borden didn't want to be disturbed and someone insisted on talking with him, I'd say that I was Borden and tell whoever I was talking with that I couldn't be disturbed."

"Did you do that often?"

"Not often, but I have done it. Usually Mr. Borden was listening on the telephone, and if he wanted to see the person, he'd cut in on the conversation. If he didn't, I'd say that he wasn't there, or that he couldn't come to the phone."

Mason moved slowly forward.

"Will you describe Dr. Callison?" he asked.

"Why, she's a woman veterinary who has a wonderful way with dogs."

"How old?"

"I'm sure I wouldn't guess at a woman's age, but she's relatively young."

"Around your age?"

"I would say she was around thirty-two or three."

"Heavy?"

"No. Very well formed."

"Surely you weren't entertaining her in your bedroom?" Mason asked, making his voice sound highly skeptical.

Ferney came up out of the witness chair angrily. "That's a lie!" he shouted.

Burger was on his feet, waving his hands. "Your Honor, Your Honor, this is uncalled for, this is completely outside of the scope of legitimate cross-examination. It is a gratuitous insult to an estimable woman. It —"

Judge Erwood pounded his gavel. "Yes, Mr. Mason," he said, "it would seem that that is certainly not called for under the circumstances."

Mason looked at the judge with an expression of wide-eyed innocence. "Why, Your Honor," he said, "it's the *only* inference to be drawn from the evidence. The witness has stated that there was a telephone in his bedroom where he slept, which was in the basement, that there was another phone in Meredith Borden's study, that when the phone rang the witness would answer, that Borden would listen in."

"But not this time," Ferney interrupted angrily. "This time *I* was answering the telephone from Borden's study."

"Oh," Mason said. "Pardon me, I didn't understand you. Then you took Dr. Callison into Borden's study, did you?"

"Yes, of course. I wouldn't have taken her down to my bedroom."

"Well," Mason said, "I beg the Court's pardon. I certainly misunderstood the witness. I thought it was quite plain from what he had said that he always answered the telephone from his bedroom."

Judge Erwood looked down at Ferney speculatively. "You certainly did give that impression in your testimony, Mr. Ferney," he said.

"Well, I didn't mean to give it. That is, that's . . . well, that's where I usually answered the phone from. But this time, because Dr. Callison was there, it was different."

"Where were you talking from?" Mason asked.

"From the study."

"Meridith Borden's study?"

"Yes."

"Let's see if we can get this straight about Dr. Callison. She is a veterinary?"

"That's right."

"And she had been treating one of the dogs?"

"Yes."

"And you were to call and get the dog?"

"Yes."

"What time?"

"Around nine o'clock."

"But you didn't call at nine o'clock?"

"No, sir."

"When did you call?"

"It was around ten-thirty."

"Why didn't you call at nine o'clock?"

"I overslept."

"You overslept?" Mason asked, his voice showing his surprise.

"All right, if you want to know," Frank Ferney said, "I was drunk. I went up to a party at the home of my fiancée and passed out."

"And who is your fiancée?"

"Loretta Harper."

Mason's brows leveled down over his eyes.

"Have you been married?"

"Yes."

"Have you ever been divorced?"

"Your Honor," Sam Drew said, "this is incompetent, irrelevant and immaterial. It is not proper cross-examination."

"On the contrary," Judge Erwood said, "this is a matter in which the Court is very much interested. The testimony of this witness indicates a most peculiar set of circumstances, and, since he is apparently being relied upon to refute the defense witness, the court wants to get at the bottom of it. Just answer the question."

"Yes, I'm married. I haven't been divorced."

"What is your wife's name?"

"She's a model. She goes under the professional name of Dawn Manning."

"All right," Mason said. "Now, let's get this straight. On this Monday night, the night of the murder, the eighth of this month, you went up to Loretta Harper's apartment. Where is that?"

"That's about a mile and a half south of Borden's place, in the town of Mesa Vista."

"What time did you go there?"

"I went there right after I had left Borden's place."

"You didn't have dinner at Borden's place?"

"No, Miss Harper had cooked dinner for two friends and myself. There was a foursome."

"And you became drunk?"

"Well, I'll change that, I didn't mean it that way. We had some cocktails before dinner and we were giving some toasts. I guess I got a little too much. I was mixing cocktails in the kitchen. There were some cocktails left in the shaker that no one wanted, and I didn't want to pour them down the sink. I very foolishly drank them, and then there was some wine with the meal and I began to get a little dizzy. I wasn't drunk, I was just feeling the liquor a little bit, and I began to get sleepy."

"So what happened?"

"I rested my head on my hand, and . . . well, I guess I went sound asleep there at the table. I was terribly embarrassed. They put me in the bedroom and I stretched out on the bed."

"With your clothes on?"

"I believe they took my shoes off, and took my coat off and hung it on the back of the chair. . . . Well, the next thing I knew, Loretta woke me up and it was then about twenty minutes past ten. Loretta had just come in and she told a story about being held up, and —"

"Never mind what anyone said," Hamilton

212

Burger interrupted ponderously. "Just describe what happened. Since Mr. Mason is so concerned with getting at this time element, we'll let him get *all* the facts."

"Well, I asked how long I'd been asleep and then I looked at my watch and suddenly remembered that I was supposed to have gone down to Dr. Callison's place to pick up this dog. I asked one of the guests to call Dr. Callison and say I'd be right down. And, believe me, I sprinted for my car."

"Which you'd left parked in front?"

"That's right. Where else would I leave it?"

Judge Erwood said, "The witness will confine himself to answering questions. There is no occasion for repartee. Counsel is simply trying to get the picture clear in his own mind, and the Court confesses that the Court wants it clarified as much as possible. Go on, Mr. Mason."

"And then?" Mason asked. "What did you do then?"

"I made time getting out to Dr. Callison's kennel. She was very nice about it. I explained to her that I'd had a little something to drink, so she took her station wagon and drove me up to Borden's house."

"What gate?"

"The back gate."

"You had a key to that?"

213

"Yes, that's close to the kennels."

"And what did you do?"

"We put the dog in the kennel, and . . . well, that was it."

Mason eyed the witness thoughtfully. "Why didn't Dr. Callison turn around and drive back in her station wagon?"

"She wanted to come in to talk with Mr. Borden."

"So you entered the house at about what time?"

"A few minutes before eleven, perhaps quarter to eleven."

"And you tried to locate Mr. Borden, didn't you?"

The witness fidgeted.

"Go ahead," Mason said. "You tried to locate Mr. Borden?"

"Well, I went in the study and he wasn't there."

"So what did you do?"

"I told Dr. Callison to sit down and I'd find him, and . . . well, I did the honors."

"What do you mean by that?"

"I bought her a drink."

"What do you mean by buying her a drink?"

"I got some liquor from the compartment back of the bar and gave her a drink."

"Did you customarily 'do the honors' for guests when Mr. Borden was not there?"

"Well, not customarily, but Dr. Callison is . . . well, sort of a privileged individual, sort of a special personage."

"I see," Mason said. "Then what happened?"

"I looked around for Mr. Borden."

"Did you call his name?"

"Yes."

"Did he answer?"

"No."

"And then what happened?"

"I can't remember a lot of details, but the burglar alarm went off, and the lights came on, and I heard the dogs barking."

"Then what?"

"Well, then I ran out and tried to find out what all the commotion was about. I whistled the dogs to me and put them in the kennels. When I came back, Dr. Callison was on the telephone talking with someone. I presume it was someone at the gate."

"Never mind your presumption," Drew interrupted.

"The Court will draw its own conclusions and presumptions, Mr. Prosecutor," Judge Erwood remarked testily. "The witness will continue."

"Well, then the phone kept ringing and ringing and ringing, so I answered, and . . . well, then I told them I was Borden."

Mason turned to the prosecutor. "I will ask the prosecution if the exposed films which were in the film holders and in the camera have been developed and printed. I believe the prosecution offered to produce prints of those."

"Do you have those prints, Mr. District Attorney?" Judge Erwood asked. "The court will be interested in viewing them."

Hamilton Burger said, "I am quite certain, if the Court please, that they have no significance as far as this case is concerned. The prosecution and the police are quite satisfied that these films had been taken at a much earlier date."

"The question," Judge Erwood said somewhat testily, "is whether you have them."

"Yes, Your Honor, we have them."

"Will you produce them, please, and give them to the Court? And I think you should show a copy to counsel for the defense."

"We are going to object to having these pictures received in evidence," Hamiliton Burger said. "We are willing to *show* them to the Court if the Court requires, but they are not proper evidence, they have no bearing on the case. We feel quite certain they were taken some days earlier."

"Why don't you want them in evidence?" Judge Erwood asked curiously.

"When the Court sees the nature of the pictures, the Court will understand," Hamilton Burger said. "The decedent was an amateur photographer. Evidently he was engaged in some sort of a friendly rivalry or contest with some other amateur photographers, and an attempt was being made to create some amateur art calendars. There is nothing actually illegal or indecent about these pictures, but they are, nevertheless, very beautiful pictures of a very beautiful woman. The Court will understand the manner in which evidence of this sort could be seized upon by the public press."

Hamilton Burger passed up a series of five-by-seven prints to the judge, then grudgingly extended a duplicate series to Perry Mason.

Mason regarded the pictures with thoughtful appraisal.

The photographs showed Dawn Manning posing in the nude against a dark background. She was turned so that her left side was toward the camera. The poses were artistic, with the left arm stretched in front of her, her right leg extended behind with the toes just touching the floor. She was leaning slightly forward. Apparently the attempt on the part of the photographer had been to capture the semblance of motion. The posing was remarkably similar to that of metallic ornaments which at one time graced the radiator caps of automobiles.

Judge Erwood raised his eyebrows over the pictures, spent some time examining them. Slowly he nodded. "These pictures are very artistic," he said. "I am going to permit them to be introduced in evidence if the defense asks to have them introduced."

"I ask they be received in evidence," Mason said.

"They prove nothing," Hamilton Burger objected.

"They may or may not prove anything," the judge ruled, "but they may be received in evidence."

"Just one more question of this witness, if the Court please," Mason said, turning to Ferney. "Have you seen those pictures?"

"No, sir."

"You'd better take a look at them, then," Judge Erwood said.

Ferney looked at the photographs which Mason extended to him. "That's Dawn!" he exclaimed. "That's my wife."

It was Mason's turn to bow to Hamilton Burger and hand him a hot potato. "That's all," he said. "I have no further questions of this witness."

Burger and Drew held a heated, whispered conference, trying to decide whether to let the witness go from the stand or to ask further questions.

Drew finally obtained seemingly reluctant consent from Hamilton Burger, and got to his feet.

"Mr. Ferney," Drew said, "just to get the essential issues in this case straight, you were the one who talked on the telephone shortly after eleven o'clock?"

"Yes, sir."

"You were the one who said you were Meridith Borden?"

"Yes, sir."

"As far as you know of your own knowledge, Meridith Borden was not alive at that time. You can't say whether he was or whether he was not?"

"That is right."

"You called his name?"

"Yes, sir."

"And he didn't answer?"

"That's right."

"And Dr. Margaret Callison was the woman who answered the telephone when it rang around eleven?"

"Yes, sir."

"Thank you," Sam Drew said. "That's all."

Mason said, "I have no further questions of this witness, but at this time, if the Court please, I desire to recall Harvey Dennison to the stand for further cross-examination."

"The manager of the Valley View Hardware

Company?" Hamilton Burger asked.

"That's right."

"Any objection?" Judge Erwood asked.

Hamilton Burger smiled. "No objection, Your Honor. Counsel can cross-examine Mr. Dennison as much as he wants to, any time he wants to."

Harvey Dennison returned to the stand.

Mason said, "Mr. Dennison, are you acquainted with a young woman by the name of Dawn Manning?"

"I am."

"Was she ever in your employ?"

"She was."

"When?"

"About three years ago she worked for us for . . . oh, about six months, I guess."

"Was Dawn Manning in your employ at the time the Colt revolver Number 613096 was found to be missing from stock?" Mason asked.

"Just a moment, just a moment, Your Honor," Hamilton Burger said. "That is not proper cross-examination, that's making an accusation by innuendo, that's completely incompetent, irrelevant and immaterial."

Judge Erwood shook his head. "The objection is overruled. Answer the question."

"She was in our employ," Dennison said.

"Dawn Manning was her maiden name?"

"It was."

"Do you know when she was married?"

"I can't give you the exact date, but she was in our employ until she married. She left our employ when she married."

"Do you know the name of the man she married?"

"I don't remember that."

"Thank you," Mason said. "That's all."

"Now, just a minute, just a minute," Hamilton Burger said, angrily. "An accusation has been made that Dawn Manning stole this gun. Do you have any evidence whatever that would lead you to believe she took the gun, Mr. Dennison?"

"None whatever," Dennison said. And then added firmly, "My opinion of Dawn Manning is that she is a very estimable —"

"Your opinion is uncalled for," Judge Erwood interrupted. "Just confine yourself to answering questions."

"Did you ever have any occasion to doubt her honesty?" Hamilton Burger asked.

"None whatever."

"That's all!" Burger snapped angrily.

Mason smiled.

"Any redirect?" Judge Erwood asked.

Mason, still smiling, said, "You have no occasion to doubt the honesty of Dawn Manning, but she was working for you at a time when the gun disappeared. Now, I will ask you this, Mr. Dennison: Did George Ansley, the defendant, ever work for you?"

"Your Honor!" Hamilton Burger shouted. "That is improper, that is misconduct, that is not proper cross-examination."

Judge Erwood smiled in spite of himself. "The question, as such, is, I believe, proper. The witness may answer it yes or no."

"No," Harvey Dennison said, "George Ansley never worked for us."

"As far as you know, was he ever in your store?"

"No."

"That's all," Mason said.

"No further questions," Hamilton Burger said, so choked up with anger that he could hardly talk.

Judge Erwood, still smiling slightly, said, "That's all, Mr. Dennison. You're excused. You may leave the stand."

Drew and Hamilton Burger conferred in whispers, than Drew got to his feet.

"It would seem, Your Honor, that despite the desperate attempts of the defense to drag another person into this case, the defendant has no alibi, and, under the circumstances, there can be none. It would seem quite apparent that Meridith Borden was lying dead in the studio, that he was killed by a weapon which was subsequently recovered from the possession of the defendant, that the defendant had threatened to kill Borden, that the defendant had the motive and the opportunity to carry out his threats. In view of the fact that this is a preliminary examination, I fail to see what more evidence needs to be supplied in order to entitle the prosecution to an order binding the defendant over."

Judge Erwood hesitated a moment, then slowly nodded.

"Just a moment," Mason said. "I don't think the case is ready for argument at this time. The prosecution was putting on rebuttal evidence."

"Well, that's all of it. That's all there is. That's our case," Drew said.

"In that case," Mason announced urbanely, "I wish to put on some further evidence of my own in surrebuttal. I want to call Loretta Harper to the stand."

"Loretta Harper will come forward and be sworn," Judge Erwood said.

Loretta Harper came forward with her chin up, her lips clamped in a line of firm determination. She took the oath and settled herself on the witness stand.

Mason said, "Your name is Loretta Harper."

"That's right."

"Where do you reside?"

"At Mesa Vista."

"That is how far from Meridith Borden's place?"

223

"About a mile and a half."

"You are acquainted with the defendant, George Ansley?"

"Until I saw him at the Borden place, I don't think I'd ever met him in my life."

"Are you acquainted with Frank Ferney?"

"I am."

"Do you know his wife, who goes under the professional name of Dawn Manning?"

"I do."

"Do you have occasion to remember the night of Monday, the eighth of this month?"

"I do, indeed."

"Will you tell us exactly what happened on that evening?"

"Objected to," Hamilton Burger said, "as incompetent, irrelevant and immaterial. What happened to *this* witness on the night of the murder has absolutely no bearing on the limited issues of the case at this time."

Judge Erwood frowned thoughtfully, then turned to Mason. "Can you narrow your question?" Erwood asked.

"With reference to what took place at the home of Meridith Borden," Mason added.

"With that addition," Judge Erwood said, "the objection is overruled."

"I do, indeed. I know exactly what happened."

"Will you please tell us," Mason said, "exactly what happened, commencing at the time you had occasion to be in or about the grounds of Meredith Borden's estate."

"I was driven through the gates," she said, "by Dawn Manning. Dawn lost control of the car. She was trying to drive with one hand and holding a gun with the other, and —"

"Just a minute, just a minute," Hamilton Burger interrupted. "If the Court please, we are now getting into something that is entirely extraneous. The answer shows plainer than any objection I could make the vice of permitting counsel to put a witness on the stand and ask a blanket question covering activities which are in no way connected with the issues before the Court."

Judge Erwood said, "*I* will ask the witness a question. What time was this, Miss Harper?"

"You mean when we entered the grounds?"

"Yes."

"It was, I would say, right around nine o'clock."

"The objection is overruled," Judge Erwood said. "The witness will be permitted to tell her story. Counsel for both sides will note that we are now dealing with events which happened on the premises when the murder took place, at a time when the expert medical testimony indicates the murder could have taken place. Under those circumstances, the defense is entitled to call any witness and ask any question that will shed light on what happened. This is a court of justice, not a gym wherein counsel may practice legal calisthenics. Proceed, Miss Harper."

"Well, Dawn Manning was driving with one hand. The other hand was holding a gun. The roads were wet, she lost control of the car and started to skid. Just at that time another car, driven by George Ansley, the defendant in this case, was coming out of the Borden place."

"And then what happened?" Mason asked.

"This car being driven by Dawn Manning ticked the front of the Ansley car and we shot through the hedge and the car turned over."

"Go on," Mason said.

"I was thrown clear of the car when it turned over. I hit with something of a jar, but it wasn't bad enough to hurt me at all. It was sort of a skid . . . that is, I slid along on the wet grass. There was a lawn. It had been raining and the grass was long and wet."

"Go on," Mason said. "What happened?"

Judge Erwood was leaning forward on the bench, his hand cupped behind his ear so that he would not miss a word.

Over at the prosecution's table, Sam Drew and Hamilton Burger were engaged in a whispered conference. It was quite evident that they were far from happy.

"Well," Loretta Harper went on, "the first thought that flashed through my mind —"

Mason held up his hand.

"We're not interested in your thoughts," Judge Erwood said. "We wanted to know what you did."

"Well, I got up and stood there for a moment, and then I saw Mr. Ansley coming with a flashlight. The flashlight, however, was giving just a faint illumination, a reddish glow, not enough to do much good."

"When you say it was Mr. Ansley coming," Mason said, "you are referring to the defendant in this case?"

"Yes, sir."

"And what did Mr. Ansley do?"

"Mr. Ansley walked around the car, and then I saw Dawn Manning lying there where she had skidded after being thrown from the car. She was unconscious."

"Then what happened?"

"Mr. Ansley started to lean over to look at her and then the light went out and it was impossible to see anything. He threw the flashlight away."

"Did you see him throw it?"

"Well, I saw his hand go back. I could dimly make that out. It was pretty dark, but I saw that, and then I saw the flash of reflected light from a nickel-plate flashlight as he threw it away, and I heard it thud when it hit the ground."

"Go on," Mason said. "Then what happened?"

"Mr. Ansley started toward the house. I knew that he was going to —"

"Never mind what you thought," Mason said. "We're only interested in what you did."

"Well, I grabbed Dawn Manning by the heels and I pulled her along the wet grass for a distance of . . . oh, I don't know, fifteen or twenty feet, almost up against the wall."

"And then what?"

"Then, I . . . well, I arranged my clothes just the way hers had been so it would look as though I had skidded along the grass, and put myself in the position she had been occupying, and shouted for help."

"Then what?"

"I waited a few seconds and shouted 'Help' again."

"Then what?"

"Then I heard steps coming toward me. Mr. Ansley was coming back. That was what I wanted."

"Go on," Mason said. "What did you do?"

"I waited until he was near enough so he could see the way I was lying, and then I straightened up and pulled my skirt down a

228

little and asked him to help me up."

"What did he do?"

"He gave me his hand and I got to my feet. He wanted to know if I was hurt and I told him no, and he said he would drive me home."

"And where was Dawn Manning all this time?" Mason asked.

"Dawn Manning," she said with acid venom, "had recovered consciousness, had regained possession of the gun and had gone —"

"Just a minute, just a minute," Hamilton Burger interrupted. "We submit, if the Court please, that the witness is testifying as to things about which she knows nothing of her own knowledge."

"Did you see Dawn Manning regain the gun?" Judge Erwood asked.

"No, sir. I only know what she must have done. It was exactly what happened. She wasn't lying there when I got to my feet. She had recovered consciousness, and —"

"Now, just a minute, just a minute," Judge Erwood interrupted. "I want you to understand, Miss Harper, that you can only testify as to things you know of your own knowledge, not as to conclusions. Now, did you see Dawn Manning recover consciousness and get to her feet?"

"No, I didn't *see* her, but by the time I got to my feet and after I had talked for a few minutes with Mr. Ansley and got him to agree to take me home, I had to walk around the front of the car, and I could look into the darkness and see that Dawn Manning was no longer where I had left her. She had recovered consciousness and moved."

"Did you see her move?"

"No, but I know she wasn't there where I had left her."

"Then that's all you can testify to," Judge Erwood said. "Proceed with your questioning, Mr. Mason."

"Did the defendant take you home?" Mason asked.

"No."

Judge Erwood looked at her with a frown. "I thought you said that he took you home."

"He thought he took me home, but he didn't."

"What do you mean by that?" Judge Erwood asked impatiently.

"I asked him to take me home and he said he would. He asked me where I lived and I told him the Ancordia Apartments, and he took me there."

"Then he took you home!" Judge Erwood snapped.

"No, sir, he did not."

The judge's face flushed.

"I think the witness means," Mason hastened to explain, "that she didn't live at the Ancordia Apartments."

"Then why did he take her there?" Judge Erwood asked.

"Because that's where she *told* him she lived."

Judge Erwood looked again at the witness. "You mean that you lied to him?"

"Yes, Your Honor."

"Why?" Judge Erwood asked.

"If the Court please," Hamilton Burger said, "with all due respect to the Court's question, I submit that we're getting into a lot of things here which are extraneous."

"Yes, I suppose so," Judge Erwood said. "After all, this is direct examination. You have the right to cross-examine. The situation seems confused to the Court. However, when we analyze the testimony of this witness, it would appear that all we have shown is that another person was perhaps at the scene of the crime —"

Judge Erwood stroked his chin thoughtfully, then turned to the witness. "You're certain that Mrs. Ferney, or Dawn Manning, as you call her, had moved before you left the grounds?"

"Absolutely certain, Your Honor, and I am certain she had gone on to Meridith Borden's house."

"Now, why do you say that?"

"She was photographed there," Loretta Harper said.

"That's a conclusion of the witness," Judge Erwood said. "It may go out of the record. There's no need for you to make the motion, Mr. District Attorney. The Court will strike that of his own motion."

Mason moved forward, presented the photographs of Dawn Manning to the witness. "Do you recognize these photographs?" he asked.

"Yes!" she snapped.

"Who is the person shown in the photographs?"

"Dawn Manning."

"State to the Court whether that is the same person you have referred to as the one who turned into Meridith Borden's estate at about nine o'clock on the night of the eighth of this month."

"That is the one."

Mason turned to the prosecution's table. "Cross-examine," he said.

Again there was a whispered conference.

At length, Hamilton Burger arose ponderously. "You don't know that Dawn Manning, as you call her, ever went near that house, do you, Miss Harper?"

"Of course I know it."

"Of your own knowledge?"

"Well, I know it as well as I know anything. Her photographs were there."

"Don't argue with me!" Hamilton Burger said, pointing his finger at the witness. "You only surmise it from these photographs, isn't that right?"

"No!" she snapped.

"No?" Hamilton Burger asked in surprise.

"That's right!" she snapped at him. "I said no!"

"You mean you have some other means of knowledge?"

"Yes."

Hamilton Burger, recognizing that he had got himself out on a limb, hesitated as to whether to ask the next logical question or to try to cover by avoiding the subject.

It was Judge Erwood who, having taken a keen personal interest in the proceedings, solved the dilemma. "If you have some other means of information," he said, "indicating Dawn Manning went to the house, and you have not disclosed that, it would be advisable for you to tell us how you know she was in the house."

"Frank Ferney knocked on the door of the studio," Loretta Harper said. "A woman said, 'Go away,' and Frank recognized her voice as the voice of his wife."

233

"How do you know that?" Hamilton Burger shouted at the witness.

"Frank told me so himself."

"I move that this statement of the witness be stricken from the record, that all of this evidence about Dawn Manning having gone to the house be stricken as a conclusion of the witness and as being founded on hearsay," Hamilton Burger said.

"The motion is granted," Judge Erwood ruled, but there was a speculative frown on his face.

"I have no further questions," Hamilton Burger said.

"No redirect," Mason said.

The witness started to leave the stand. "Just a moment," Judge Erwood said. "This is a most peculiar situation. The Court is, of course, keenly aware that under the law, evidence is restricted so that extraneous evidence and hearsay evidence is not admitted in Court. But here we have a most unusual situation. The Court is going to ask a few questions to try to clarify the matter somewhat."

The judge turned to the witness. "Miss Harper, you stated that Dawn Manning was driving the car."

"Yes, sir, Your Honor."

"With one hand?"

"Yes, sir."

"And the other hand was holding a gun?"

"Yes, sir."

"Where was that gun pointed?"

"At me."

"How did it happen that you were riding in the car with Dawn Manning?"

"She forced me to get in at the point of a gun."

"Then she had a gun with her all of the time?"

"Yes, Your Honor."

"Of course, you have no means of knowing whether this was the gun which, according to the testimony of the ballistics expert, was the weapon from which the fatal bullet was fired."

Loretta Harper said, "It *looked* like the same gun. She stole the car, and she could just as easily have stolen the gun. Frank Ferney has been trying to protect her. Make *him* tell what happened."

Judge Erwood said hastily, "Well now, of course, we are getting into a lot of extraneous matters. That last remark is legally irrelevant. However, what appears to have been a rather simple case now becomes more complicated. Do you have any more questions, Mr. Prosecutor?"

"None," Burger said.

"Mr. Mason?"

"None," Mason said.

"The witness is excused."

Mason said, "I now desire to recall Mr. Ferney for further cross-examination."

"That is objected to, if the Court please," Hamilton Burger said. "The prosecution has concluded its case, the defense had ample opportunity to cross-examine Mr. Ferney, and covered his testimony thoroughly."

"The Court feels that it understands the question Mr. Mason wants to ask of Mr. Ferney," Judge Erwood said. "And, since the order of proof in motions of this sort are addressed to the sound discretion of the Court, the Court will grant the motion. In fact, the Court will state that if Mr. Mason has not made this motion, the Court of its own motion would have asked Mr. Ferney to return to the stand.

"The motion is granted, Mr. Mason. Mr. Ferney, return to the stand."

Ferney came forward and took the witness stand.

"Go ahead, Mr. Mason, resume your cross-examination."

Mason said, "Directing your attention to the time when you have testified that you were looking for Meridith Borden after you and Dr. Callison had entered the house, did you go up the stairs to the room used as a photographic studio?"

"I did."

"Was the door open or closed?"

"It was closed."

"Did you knock on that door?"

"Yes."

"What happened?"

"A woman's voice called out, 'Go away.' "

"Why didn't you tell us about this before?"

"Because I wasn't asked."

"Weren't you asked if you had tried to locate Borden and had been unable to do so, if you had called his name and had received no answer?"

"I called his name. I received no answer. I told the truth."

"But now you say there was a woman in the studio."

"Sure. Lots of times women were there. This is the first time anyone asked me about her."

"And she said, 'Go away'?"

"Yes."

"Now then," Mason said, "I ask you if you know of your own knowledge who the woman was who was on the other side of that closed door?"

Ferney hesitated, then said in a low voice, "I feel that I do."

"Who was it?"

237

"It was my wife, Dawn."

"You mean the woman who has been variously described as Dawn Manning and as Mrs. Frank Ferney?"

"That is correct."

"She was your wife?"

"Yes, sir."

"That is all," Mason said.

"I have no questions," Hamilton Burger said.

"Now, just a moment," Judge Erwood said. "The Court dislikes to be placed in the position of carrying on the examination of witnesses, but certainly there is a situation here which is most unusual. Mr. Ferney?"

"Yes, Your Honor."

"When you gave your testimony before, why didn't you state that you heard the voice of a woman on the other side of that door in the studio?"

"No one asked me."

"You made no attempt to open the door?"

"No, sir."

"Was it locked?"

"I don't know."

"Isn't it unusual that a person should hear the voice of his wife on the other side of the door and simply turn away without making any attempt to open the door?"

"No, Your Honor. That door had to be kept

closed. One never knew whether the darkroom was in use, or whether the studio was being used for photographic purposes. I was working for Meridith Borden. If I had opened the door at that time, he would have fired me on the spot.

"I also wish to point out to the Court that my wife and I have separated, and the fact that we have not been formally divorced was entirely due to my fault."

"In what way was it your fault?" Judge Erwood asked.

"I went to Reno and established a residence. I was supposed to get the divorce. The case was ready to be disposed of, but I got in an argument with my lawyer. I felt he was trying to hold me up. I simply sat tight and decided to outwait him."

Judge Erwood looked at Ferney with a puzzled expression. "I feel this matter should be clarified," he said, shifting his glance to the district attorney.

"We have no further questions," Burger said doggedly.

Judge Erwood's face showed annoyance. He turned to Perry Mason.

Mason bowed to the Court. "With the Court's permission," he said, and arose to walk toward the witness stand, facing the discomfited witness. "Let's get your own time

schedule on the night of the murder straight,"
he said. "You say you left Borden's house a
little after six o'clock?"

"Yes."

"And you went where?"

"To the apartment of Loretta Harper, my
fiancée."

"Did your fiancée, as you call her, know
that you were not divorced?"

"Not at that time. She thought I was divorced."

"You lied to her?"

Ferney flushed, and for a moment started
to make some hot rejoinder, then caught himself.

"You lied to her?" Mason repeated.

"All right," Ferney said defiantly, "I lied
to her."

"Who was present when you arrived at the
apartment of Miss Harper?"

"Just Loretta Harper."

"Later on, other people came in?"

"Yes."

"How much later?"

"About fifteen or twenty minutes later."

"Who were these people?"

"Mr. and Mrs. Jason Kendell."

"And how long did they remain?"

"They remained until . . . well, until quite
late, until Loretta — I mean Miss Harper —

got back from having been kidnaped."

"Now, when you say kidnaped, what do you mean?"

"If the Court please," Hamilton Burger said, "I feel that this witness can't possibly know what transpired with Miss Harper —"

"I'm not asking him what transpired," Mason said. "I'm asking him to simply define what he meant by the use of the term kidnaped."

"The witness is presumed to understand the ordinary meaning of the words he uses," Judge Erwood said. "The objection is sustained."

"All right," Mason said to the witness, "you went to this apartment. What floor is it on?"

"The fourth."

"You had some drinks?"

"Yes."

"And you had dinner?"

"Yes."

"And then you became a little dizzy?"

"Quite dizzy."

"You were intoxicated?"

"I was intoxicated, yes."

"And then what happened?"

"I went to sleep at the table."

"What do you know after that? How much do you remember?"

"I have a vague recollection of being placed on the bed."

"Who did that?"

"Jason and Millicent — that is, Mr. and Mrs. Kendell assisted by Miss Harper. I remember they took my shoes off and that's the last I remember until I woke up because I heard a lot of excitement — that is, excited voices, and looked at my watch."

"Were you intoxicated at the time?"

"No, I'd slept it off. I had a thick feeling in my head."

"And, at that time, Miss Harper was back in the apartment?"

"That's right."

"So then you called this veterinary, Dr. Callison?"

"I didn't wait to call her. I asked one of the others to call and say that I was on my way, and I made a dash for my automobile. I drove to the kennels."

"That's all," Mason said.

Loretta Harper jumped up from her seat in the courtroom. "Tell them the truth, Frank," she shouted. "Quit trying to protect her! Mr. Mason, ask him what he told Dr. Callison! He heard —"

"That will do!" Judge Erwood said, banging his gavel. "Miss Harper, come forward."

Loretta Harper came forward, her face flushed with indignation.

"Don't you know that you're not supposed

to rise in court and shout comments of that sort?" Judge Erwood asked.

"I can't help it, Your Honor. He's still concealing things, still trying to stick up for her. He heard —"

"Now, just a minute," Judge Erwood said. "This situation is getting entirely out of hand. I am not interested in any further comments from you, Miss Harper. If you know anything about the case of your own knowledge, that's one thing, but this Court certainly doesn't care to have interpolations from spectators. Now, the Court is going to hold you in contempt of this Court for interrupting the proceedings in this case and comporting yourself in a manner which you knew was improper. The Court will determine the extent of the punishment later. But in the meantime, you're to consider yourself held in contempt of Court and you are technically in custody. Do you understand that?"

"Yes, sir."

"Call me Your Honor."

"Yes, Your Honor."

"Very well. Be seated now and keep quiet."

Judge Erwood turned angrily to Frank Ferney. "Mr. Ferney," he said, "you're under oath. You are called here to tell the truth, the whole truth and nothing but the truth. Now, you've certainly placed yourself in a most unfavorable light, not only by your testimony but by the manner in which you've given that testimony. The Court is thoroughly out of patience with you. Now, is there anything else that you know, anything at all that you know of your own knowledge that would shed any light on this matter?"

Ferney lowered his eyes.

"Yes or no?" Judge Erwood asked.

"Yes," Ferney said.

"All right, what is it?" Judge Erwood snapped.

Ferney said, "As we were leaving, driving away from the place, I thought I heard . . . well, I could have been mistaken about that. I —"

"What did you think you heard?" Judge Erwood asked.

"I thought I heard a shot."

"A shot!"

"Yes."

Judge Erwood glowered at the witness.

"Did you mention this to Dr. Callison?" Mason asked.

"We object," Burger snapped.

"Sustained."

"You were riding in the car with Dr. Callison?" Mason asked.

"Yes."

"You rode back to the kennels with her?"

"Yes."

"What time did you reach there?"

"Around eleven-thirty or perhaps a little after."

"And you then picked up your own car there?"

"Yes."

"And returned to your room at the Borden place?"

The witness fidgeted. "No. I didn't stay there that night."

"That's all," Mason announced.

"Any further direct examination?" Judge Erwood asked Hamilton Burger.

"No, Your Honor."

"The witness is excused," Judge Erwood said, "but don't leave the courtroom. The Court feels that your conduct has been reprehensible. You have endeavored to conceal facts from the Court."

Mason said, "If the Court please, there *is* one further question I would like to ask, a question by way of impeachment."

"Go ahead," Judge Erwood said.

Mason said, "Unfortunately, Your Honor, I can't lay a foundation by giving the exact time and the exact place or the exact persons present, but I can ask a general impeaching question. Isn't it a fact, Mr. Ferney, that at some time after the night of Monday, the eighth of this month, you told Loretta Harper that you knew your wife had murdered Meridith Borden and that you were going to try to protect her if you could?"

"Just a moment, just a moment!" Hamilton Burger shouted, getting to his feet. "That question is improper, it's improper cross-examination, it's objected to."

"What's improper about it as cross-examination?" Judge Erwood snapped.

Hamilton Burger, caught off balance, hesitated.

Sam Drew jumped to his feet. "If the Court please, no proper foundation has been laid. A question of that sort should specify the exact time and the persons present. Moreover, the opinion of this witness is of absolutely no value."

Judge Erwood said, "Counsel has stated that he doesn't know the time; that he doesn't know who was present. He has, however, asked the witness specifically if he didn't have a certain conversation with Loretta Harper. The object of that question is not to prove the fact, but to prove the motivation of the witness, his animosity toward any of the parties, his reason for concealing testimony. I'm going to let him answer the question."

The judge turned to Ferney. "Answer the question."

Ferney twisted and squirmed on the chair.

"Well, I . . . I may have said —"

"Yes or no?" Judge Erwood snapped. "Did you make such a statement?"

"Well, yes, I did. I told her that."

"That's all," Mason said.

"That's all," Hamilton Burger said, his manner showing his extreme annoyance.

Judge Erwood said, "The witness is excused."

Mason said, "If the court please, I would like to have a subpoena issued for Dr. Margaret Callison, and I would ask the Court to grant the defense a continuance until such a subpoena can be served."

"Any objection on the part of the prosecution?" Judge Erwood asked.

"Yes, Your Honor," Sam Drew said. "In the first place, counsel has had ample opportunity to prepare his case. In the second place, the case in chief has all been submitted. The prosecution has rested its case, the defense has rested its case, the prosecution has called rebuttal witnesses, the issues are limited at this time."

Judge Erwood looked down at Mason, said, "The Court is going to take a ten-minute recess, Mr. Mason, and, at the end of that recess, the Court will rule on your motion."

Mason pushed his way through the crowd of spectators to catch Paul Drake's arm. "Get a subpoena, Paul. Serve it on Dr. Callison. Get her here. Rush!"

"You don't think he's going to give you a continuance so you can get her here?" Drake asked.

"I don't know," Mason said. "I *think* he's giving me an opportunity to get her here without granting the continuance. I don't know. Judge Erwood, of course, was planning to shut me off and show me that this was only a preliminary hearing, and I couldn't pull any of my legal pyrotechnics here. Now he's interested, and — Get started, Paul. Get going."

"On my way," Drake said.

"Bring her back with you," Mason told him, "and rush it."

Drake nodded and pushed his way out of the courtroom.

Mason turned back to where Della Street was standing.

"Well?" she asked.

Mason said, "I'm darned if I know, Della. There's something here that is very peculiar."

"I think it's plain as can be," she said. "Frank Ferney is trying to protect his wife, or, rather, was trying to protect her, and that made Loretta Harper furious."

Mason said, "There's something back of all this. Della, what would you do if you were a crooked politician, if you adopted the position that you were only a public relations expert, that you wouldn't think of acting as intermediary in the taking of bribes, that you would act only in a consulting capacity — and then you took in large sums of money which, in turn, you passed out as bribes?"

Della Street made a little grimace. "I'd probably kill myself about the second night. I don't think I could sleep in the same bed with myself."

"But suppose you got to the point where you were putting up with yourself and making a very good living out of what you were doing?"

"What are you getting at?" she asked.

Mason said, "Borden undoubtedly took some steps to protect himself. He knew that when Ansley called on him, Ansley felt he was passing out bribe money. Borden had to accept that money and he had to use it as bribe money. But, in order to keep his skirts clean, he had to adopt the position that he was acting legitimately as a public relations counselor.

"Under those circumstances, if I were Borden, I would keep a tape recording of every conversation which took place and be able to produce those tape recordings if I ever got in a jam."

"Well?" she asked.

"No one has said anything about a tape re-

249

cording of the Ansley conversation."

"Would you want one?" she asked. "Would it help your client?"

"There's one way," Mason said, "in which it would help my client a lot."

"What? I'm afraid I don't understand."

"If Ansley went there to kill him," Mason said, "he wouldn't first employ him as a public relations counselor, and *then* kill him."

"But he might have become angered after having the conversation."

"He might have," Mason said, grinning, "but there's one very significant matter which I think our friends on the prosecution have overlooked. . . . Where's Lieutenant Tragg? Is he around?"

"Yes, he's sitting in court taking in all the testimony."

"Fine," Mason said, grinning. "Tragg will tell the truth."

Chapter 11

When Judge Erwood returned to the bench, Hamilton Burger arose to renew his objection.

"If the Court please," he said, "if the defense had wanted to call Dr. Callison as a witness, they should have had her under subpoena.

"I think it is quite apparent to this Court that what the defense is doing is merely going on a general fishing expedition, trying to call as many witnesses as possible, trying to find out what they know about the case, trying to get them on the record so that the defense counselor will have a record from which to impeach their testimony when they get into the superior court.

"I know that Courts don't approve of these tactics generally, and I think this Court will agree with me that there has been a tendency in the past to transform some preliminary hearings into spectacular trials which go far outside the issues that should have been determined at a preliminary examination."

"You are continuing to resist the motion for a continuance so that Dr. Callison can be subpoenaed?" Judge Erwood asked.

"Exactly, Your Honor. And may I point out further that the case has now reached the point of rebuttal and surrebuttal. If counsel wishes a continuance in order to serve this subpoena, counsel should make a formal motion, supported by an affidavit stating exactly what it is he expects Dr. Callison to state once she is sworn as a witness. Quite obviously, counsel can't do that, because counsel is simply engaged in exploring the possibilities of the situation by calling every witness he feels may ultimately be called as a witness for the prosecution in the higher court."

Mason, smiling urbanely, said, "Well, if the Court please, we can debate that point a little later. Right at the moment, I have another witness I wish to recall for further cross-examination."

Burger's face darkened. "There you are, Your Honor. Counsel is simply stalling. He undoubtedly has sent out to have Dr. Callison subpoenaed, and now he'll recall witness after witness for cross-examination, simply stalling around until Dr. Callison can get here."

"What witness do you wish to recall for further cross-examination?" Judge Erwood asked.

"Lieutenant Tragg, Your Honor."

"This motion is addressed to the sound discretion of the Court. You have heard the charge made by the district attorney that the purpose of this motion is simply to gain time by a long, drawn-out cross-examination, Mr. Mason."

"Yes, Your Honor."

"Are you prepared to deny that charge?"

Mason grinned and said, "Not in its entirety, Your Honor. I hope to have Dr. Callison here by the time I have finished with Lieutenant Tragg's cross-examination. But I will further state to the Court that I am not asking to recall the witness for further cross-examination simply to gain time. I have a definite purpose in mind."

"What is that purpose?" Judge Erwood asked.

"I think, if the Court please," Mason said, "the purpose will become readily apparent as soon as I start questioning the witness. Naturally, I do not want to give my hand away by showing the prosecution my trump cards."

Judge Erwood frowned thoughtfully, then said, "Lieutenant Tragg will come forward for further cross-examination. The Court will state that this cross-examination must be brief and to the point, and the Court will not permit what is generally referred to as a fishing expedition on the part of counsel.

"Lieutenant Tragg, come forward, please."

Lt. Tragg resumed the witness stand.

"Proceed, Mr. Mason," Judge Erwood said. And, from the manner in which he was leaning forward, it was quite evident that the judge intended to enforce his ruling that there be no attempt on the part of Mason to stall for time by a long, drawn-out cross-examination.

Mason said, "You have described what you found at the scene of the murder, Lieutenant Tragg, and you have described what you found in the studio where the body was found?"

"Yes, sir."

"I will now ask you, Lieutenant Tragg, if it isn't a fact that when you examined the study or office of Meridith Borden, you found something which had considerable significance in your own mind, but which has been suppressed at this examination."

Tragg frowned.

"Your Honor, I resent that," Hamilton Burger said. "I think that constitutes misconduct. Nothing has been suppressed."

"You're willing to state that?" Mason asked Hamilton Burger.

"Certainly, sir!"

Mason grinned at Lt. Tragg's evident discomfiture. "Let's hear what the witness has to say in answer to the question," he said.

Judge Erwood started to make some impatient rejoinder, then, turning to look at Tragg's face, suddenly checked himself and leaned toward the witness.

Tragg said uncomfortably, "I'm not certain that I know what you mean by the word suppressed."

"Let me ask it this way," Mason said. "Isn't it a fact that something was found which you felt had evidentiary value and that you were instructed to say nothing about it while you were being examined in court?"

"Your Honor, I object," Hamilton Burger shouted. "This is not proper cross-examination, it is not proper surrebuttal, no proper foundation has been laid, the witness hasn't been asked who is supposed to have instructed him to say nothing and the article hasn't been described."

Mason, now sure of his ground, smiled and said, "I will supplement that with another question, if the Court please."

"You withdraw your prior question?"

"Yes, Your Honor."

"Very well, go ahead."

"Isn't it a fact, Lieutenant Tragg, that when you searched the study of the decedent, Meridith Borden, you found a concealed microphone leading to a recording device of some sort, and isn't it a fact that on that recording device you found a recording of the conversation between Meridith Borden and George Ansley? And isn't it a fact that Hamilton Burger suggested to you that you should make no mention of that recording in the preliminary examination?"

"Your Honor," Hamilton Burger said, "we object on the ground that there are several questions here, that this is not proper cross-examination, not proper surrebuttal, and —"

Judge Erwood interrupted. "Ask your questions one at a time, Mr. Mason."

Mason said, "When you were examining the premises, you looked through the study of Meridith Borden, Lieutenant Tragg?"

"Yes, sir."

"Did you find a concealed microphone in there?"

"Yes, sir."

"Did that microphone lead to, or was it connected with, a recording device of some sort?"

"Yes, sir."

"Did you find a record on that recording device?"

"Yes, sir."

"Did that record contain a recording of the complete conversation between George Ansley and Meridith Borden?"

"I don't know."

"It contained, or purported to contain, a recording of that conversation?"

"Well, *a* recording of *a* conversation."

"And isn't it a fact that Hamilton Burger told you that you were not to mention this recording at the preliminary hearing?"

"Now, just a moment, Your Honor," Hamilton Burger said. "Before the witness answers that question, I want to interpose an objection that it is argumentative, that it is incompetent, irrelevant and immaterial, that it is not proper cross-examination, that it is not proper sur-rebuttal, and that it calls for hearsay testimony."

"As the question is now asked," Judge Erwood said, "it may call for hearsay evidence. However, in view of the prosecution's indignant denial that anything had been suppressed, it would seem that this objection is somewhat technical. However, the Court will sustain the objection on the ground that it is hearsay. That objection, Mr. Mason, is to the question *in its present form.*"

"I understand, Your Honor," Mason said, noticing the emphasis which Judge Erwood placed on the last words. "I will ask the question this way: Lieutenant Tragg, why did you not mention this recorded conversation when you gave your testimony here in court?"

"Objected to as incompetent, irrelevant and

immaterial, and not proper cross-examination," Hamilton Burger said.

"In the present form of the question, the objection is overruled."

"Well, I wasn't asked about it."

"You were asked about certain things you found in the room in question?"

"Yes, sir."

"And you described the things you had found?"

"Yes, sir."

"Now in your own mind, Lieutenant, was there an intention to avoid mentioning this tape recording unless you were specifically asked about it?"

"That is objected to, Your Honor," Hamilton Burger said. "It is argumentative, it is not proper cross-examination."

"The objection is overruled!" Judge Erwood snapped. "As the question is now asked, it is eminently proper because it tends to show bias on the part of a witness. Questions are always pertinent for the purpose of showing bias. Answer the question, Lieutenant Tragg."

"Well, I made up my mind I would avoid saying anything about it unless the specific question was asked."

"And did you reach that decision in your own mind, Lieutenant, purely because of instructions which had been given you by the district attorney?"

"I object," Hamilton Burger said. "If the Court please —"

Judge Erwood shook his head. "Your objection is overruled, Mr. Burger. The question now goes entirely to the state of mind of the witness. If it appears that the witness reached a decision not to mention certain things because he had been asked by the prosecutor not to mention them, that shows bias on the part of the witness which not only can properly be disclosed by direct questions, but the Court may state that it is a matter of considerable interest to the Court. Answer the question, Lieutenant."

Lt. Tragg hesitated a moment, then said, "Yes, I was instructed to say nothing about it unless I was asked."

Mason, following up his advantage, said, "The only reason that caused you to determine to say nothing about that recording unless you were specifically asked about it was an admonition which had been given you by the district attorney. Is that right?"

"Same objection," Hamilton Burger said.

"Overruled," Judge Erwood snapped. "Answer the question."

"That's right."

"Now then," Mason said, "I feel that in the

interests of justice, we should have the recording of that interview played to the Court."

"If counsel wants to put it on as part of his case," Hamilton Burger said, "let him get the recording, bring it in and offer it, and then we will make an objection on the ground that it is completely incompetent, that this Court is not bound by two unidentified voices on a tape recording."

"Where is that recording now?" Mason asked Lt. Tragg.

"I turned it over to the district attorney."

Mason said, "I ask that the district attorney be ordered to produce that recording, and that it be played to the Court. I think that this conversation between the defendant and Meridith Borden may be of great importance. The charge is that the defendant killed Meridith Borden. Quite obviously, one doesn't have a conversation with a dead man."

Hamilton Burger, on his feet, said angrily, "There's no reason why he can't have a conversation with a man and then shoot him. That tape recording shows that he had every reason to murder Meridith Borden."

"Then it should be a part of your case," Mason said.

"I'm the sole judge of what is a part of my case," Hamilton Burger said. "All I need to do at this time is to show that a murder was committed and then produce evidence which will convince this Court that there is reasonable grounds to believe the defendant committed that murder."

"I think that is correct," Judge Erwood said. "However, the situation is now somewhat different. The defense counsel is calling upon the prosecution to produce that tape recording as a part of the *defendant's* case. The Court is going to grant that motion. That is, that the tape, or whatever the recording was on, will be played to the Court. The Court admits that this case is taking a peculiar turn and the Court is interested in finding out what actually happened."

"All of Mr. Mason's cases take peculiar turns," Hamilton Burger said angrily.

"That will do, Mr. Prosecutor. If you have that tape recording in your possession, produce it."

"It will take a few minutes to get it here and set up so we can play it."

"How long?"

"At least half an hour."

"Then the Court will take a recess for half an hour."

Drew tugged at Hamilton Burger's coattails, and, as the district attorney bent over, Drew whispered vehemently.

"Just a moment, just a moment," Hamilton

Burger said suddenly. "I'll try to have everything set up and get it here within ten minutes."

Judge Erwood looked at Burger thoughtfully. "You said it would take half an hour, Mr. Prosecutor."

"I find, on consulting with my associate, that the tape recorder is immediately available and we can get the tape here, I think, within ten minutes."

"Is that what your associate whispered to you?" Mason asked. "Or did he whisper to you that a half-hour delay would enable me to get Dr. Callison here?"

Hamilton Burger turned angrily. "You mind your business and I'll mind —"

Judge Erwood's gavel banged on the desk. "That will do, gentlemen," he said. "We will have no further exchange of personalities between counsel. However, Mr. Prosecutor, the Court was not born yesterday. You said that it would take half an hour to get the recording here, and the Court made an order that the Court would recess for thirty minutes. The Court sees no reason to change that order. The recess will be for thirty minutes."

And Judge Erwood got up from the bench and stalked angrily into chambers.

Chapter 12

Five minutes before court reconvened, Paul Drake came hurrying into the courtroom, accompanied by a trim-looking woman.

Mason beckoned them over to the defense counsel table where he was seated in conversation with George Ansley.

"This is Dr. Margaret Callison, the veterinary," Paul Drake said, "and this is Perry Mason, the lawyer for Ansley."

"How do you do, Mr. Mason," she said, giving him her hand and a warm smile. "I've read about you for a long time. I hardly expected to meet you. I told Mr. Drake that I don't believe I know a thing that has any bearing on what happened."

"Perhaps if you'll tell me exactly what happened," Mason said, "we can correlate your story with other facts in the case, and perhaps find something which will be of value. I have subpoenaed you as a witness and I want you to stand by, but I may not have to put you on the stand. Tell me what happened."

She said, "I had one of the Borden dogs for treatment. Mr. Borden liked to have the dogs there at night. They would be brought in early in the morning, as a rule. I would treat them during the day and he would come for them at night."

"And on this particular Monday?" Mason asked.

"I had one of the dogs which had been delivered at eight o'clock in the morning. I treated the dog, and Mr. Ferney was to come for it at nine o'clock that night.

"When he didn't come, I waited around for his call, feeling that he had probably been detained. Actually, that call didn't come until right around ten-twenty-five, and then it wasn't Mr. Ferney who called. It was a man who said he was calling for Mr. Ferney, that Mr. Ferney had been unavoidably detained. He asked me if I could have the dog ready, despite the lateness of the hour. The man said Mr. Ferney was on his way."

"You agreed?"

"Yes, I told him I would have the dog in my station wagon; that it would take me about five minutes to get the dog and load it."

"You did that?"

"That's right."

"And when did Frank Ferney arrive?"

"Just after I had the dog loaded in my station

264

wagon. He parked his car in front of my place, and I drove the station wagon to Borden's place."

"How far are you from the Borden place?"

"Only a little over two miles."

"Then what happened?" Mason asked.

"Well, we went up to the gate, Mr. Ferney opened the gate with a key, and took the dog from me.

"I told him that I wanted to talk with Mr. Borden about the dog's condition. I thought an operation might be advisable. There are a couple of glands which have a tendency to become calcified, and the dog was no longer a young dog. I suggested to Mr. Ferney that it would be well to discuss the matter with Mr. Borden, and he said that I should come on in with him, and I probably would have a chance to talk to Mr. Borden."

"Then what?"

"Well, we entered the house, and Ferney said Mr. Borden wasn't in his study, he thought he was up in the studio; he'd go to look for him, and —"

The clerk pounded with his gavel. "Everybody stand up, please."

Mason whispered hastily to Dr. Callison as Judge Erwood entered the court. "When you left, did Ferney go with you?"

"Yes."

"Was he alone or out of your sight any time there in the building?"

"Not in the building. The burglar alarm came on, and he went out to call the dogs back and turn out the lights. That was when I answered the phone and said I didn't think Mr. Borden wished to be disturbed. I felt someone had been tampering with the gates, some idle curiosity seeker. I knew I shouldn't intrude on Mr. Borden wherever he was."

"But was Ferney out of your sight while he was *inside* the house?"

"Only when he went up the short flight of stairs to knock on the door of the studio."

"Did you hear him knock?"

"Yes."

"Did you hear any voices?"

"No."

"Could he have entered the room?"

"Heavens, no! There wasn't time. I heard him knock and then he came right back down. I'll tell you this, Mr. Mason, when he came down those stairs, he looked as if someone had jolted him back on his heels. He told me Borden was in the studio and didn't want to be disturbed. He said —"

The bailiff shouted, "Silence in the court! You may be seated," as Judge Erwood seated himself on the bench and glanced at the district attorney.

"The tape recording is ready, Mr. District Attorney?"

"Yes, Your Honor. I again desire to object to it on the ground that it is inadmissible, that it is not the best evidence, that it is not properly authenticated, that it is completely incompetent, irrelevant and immaterial at this time and is no part of rebuttal or surrebuttal."

"The tape recording is the actual recording that was found in the Borden residence?"

"Yes, Your Honor."

"Then the objections are overruled. We will hear the recording."

With poor grace, Hamilton Burger turned on the tape recording. For some ten minutes the recording played the voices of George Ansley and Meridith Borden.

Then the voice of Ansley coming through the loudspeaker, said, "Well, I guess I'll be getting on."

Borden's voice said, "I'm glad you dropped in, Ansley, and I'll take care of you to the best of my ability. I feel quite certain you won't have any more trouble with the inspectors. They don't like adverse publicity any better than anyone else, and, after all, I'm a public relations expert."

Borden's laugh was ironic.

"I can find my way out all right," Ansley's voice said.

"No, no, I'll see you to the door. I'm all alone here tonight. Sorry."

The tape recorder ran on for some ten seconds, then a peculiar thudding sound registered on the tape. After that, abruptly the noises ceased, although the spools of the tape recorder continued to revolve.

Hamilton Burger moved over and shut off the tape recorder, started rewinding the spools.

"That's it, Your Honor," he said.

Judge Erwood was frowning thoughtfully. "The series of crackling noises which came from the tape recorder after the voices had ceased are caused by what, Mr. District Attorney?"

"The fact that the tape recorder was continuing to run with a live microphone."

"And that muffled sound?"

"That was the sound of the shot that killed Meridith Borden," Hamilton Burger said. And then added with apparent heat, "We feel, if the Court please, that this is forcing us unnecessarily to show our hand. We had intended to produce this evidence in the superior court when the defendant was held for trial."

"Well, the defense has a right to produce it," Judge Erwood said. "I believe it is being produced on order of the Court in response to a demand by the defendant and as a part of the defendant's case."

"Well, the defendant has heard it now," Hamilton Burger said with ill grace. "And, doubtless, when he finally gets on the witness stand to tell his story in front of a jury, he will have thought up the proper answers, or they will have been thought up for him."

"There is no occasion for that comment, Mr. District Attorney," Judge Erwood said. "The defense in any case is entitled to present evidence to a Court."

"In this case," Hamilton Burger said, still angry and still insistent, "they're presenting the prosecution's case."

"We won't argue the matter!" Judge Erwood snapped. "Are there any further witnesses, Mr. Mason?"

"Yes, Your Honor," Mason said, "I desire to have Mr. Ferney recalled to the stand for further cross-examination."

"We object," Hamilton Burger said. "The defense in this case has done nothing but recall witnesses for cross-examination. The law does not contemplate that a defendant can cross-examine a witness piecemeal. The defendant is supposed to conduct his cross-examination and be finished with it."

"Anything further, Mr. Prosecutor?" Judge Erwood asked.

"No, Your Honor, that covers my position."

"Objection is overruled. The examination of witnesses is within the province of the Court. Mr. Ferney, you will return to the witness stand."

Ferney, obviously ill at ease, returned to the witness stand.

"Directing your attention to the night of the eighth of this month, at a time when you were at the Borden residence with Dr. Callison present, the time being shortly after eleven o'clock in the evening, did you state to Dr. Callison that you had climbed the stairs to the studio where Mr. Borden carried on his photographic work, and that Mr. Borden had told you he didn't want to be disturbed, or words to that effect?"

"That's objected to as hearsay and not proper cross-examination," Hamilton Burger said.

"Overruled!" Judge Erwood snapped. "It's an impeaching question. The Court is going to hear the conversation."

"But it certainly can't be binding on the prosecution anything that this witness *said*, Your Honor."

"It may not be binding on the prosecution, but it shows the attitude and the bias of this witness. The Court is going to permit the question. Go ahead and answer, Mr. Ferney."

"Well," Ferney said, "I went up the stairs

to the studio. I knocked on the door —"

"That's not the question," Judge Erwood interrupted. "The question is what you told Dr. Callison."

"Well, I told her that Mr. Borden was up in the studio taking pictures and that he didn't want to be disturbed."

"Did you say he *told* you he didn't want to be disturbed?" Mason asked.

Ferney looked over to where Dr. Callison was seated in the courtroom. "I don't remember exactly what words I used."

"After you left the house with Dr. Callison in her station wagon, did you ask her if she had heard a shot?"

"I think what I said was a noise like a shot."

"You asked her that?"

"I may have."

"That's all," Mason said.

"I have no further questions," Hamilton Burger said.

"That rests our case, Your Honor," Mason said.

"I have no further evidence, Your Honor," Hamilton Burger said. "I now move the Court to bind the defendant over to the superior court. Regardless of what the record may show as to contradictions, the fact remains that the defendant had the fatal weapon in his possession, the defendant had threatened the decedent, and, furthermore, it is apparent that the defendant fired the shot which killed the decedent within a few seconds after the termination of the interview, and apparently while the decedent was showing the defendant to the door. The sound of that shot is quite apparent on the tape recorder."

Judge Erwood frowned at the district attorney. "Is it your contention that Mr. Borden was showing him to the front door through the photographic studio?"

"Not necessarily, Your Honor."

"Then how did it happen that his body was found in the photographic studio?"

"It could have been taken there, Your Honor."

Judge Erwood turned to Perry Mason. "The Court will hear from you, Mr. Mason."

Mason said urbanely, "What happened, Your Honor, was that when Meridith Borden escorted George Ansley to the door, he slammed the front door. And it was that muffled slamming of the front door which made the sound on the tape recorder. The proof that Meridith Borden was alive after George Ansley left the house is that he returned and *immediately* shut off the tape recorder. It is quite apparent on the tape itself that the tape recorder was shut off."

"Do you question that, Mr. District Attor-

272

ney?" Judge Erwood asked the prosecutor.

Burger said, "It's quite apparent that the tape was shut off shortly after the sound of the shot, but it was the murderer, George Ansley, who shut off that tape recorder."

Judge Erwood looked at Mason. Mason smiled and shook his head.

"George Ansley didn't know where the tape recorder was," he said. "He didn't know the interview was being recorded. The tape recorder was in another room. It was necessary for the tape recorder to be shut off by someone who knew that it was on and who knew exactly where the tape recorder was located. Ansley didn't have that knowledge and couldn't have done it.

"There is, if the Court please, one other most persuasive circumstance. The Court will notice that the inspectors on the job the next day were more than courteous. Now, that means just one thing. It means that Meridith Borden had been in communication with the inspectors. Since we have now heard a complete tape recording of the interview with George Ansley, we know that at no time during that interview did Meridith Borden go to the telephone, ring up an inspector and say, in effect, 'It's all right. George Ansley has called on me and is going to kick through. You can take off the pressure.'

273

"Or, since Meridith Borden is dead and cannot refute any charge against him, perhaps I should express it this way: He didn't go to the telephone and say to the inspector, 'George Ansley has just called on me and has retained me as a public relations expert. I feel that your inspection on this construction job has been far more rigorous than is required by the contract, and represents some personal animosity on your part, or an attempt to get some kind of a bribe or kickback. Therefore, unless the situation is changed immediately, I am going to take steps to see that publicity is given the type of inspection to which Mr. Ansley has been subjected.' "

For a moment Judge Erwood's angry face relaxed into something of a smile. "A very tactful expression of a purely hypothetical conversation, Mr. Mason."

"Out of deference to the fact that Borden is now deceased and is not in a position to defend himself," Mason said.

Judge Erwood looked down at the prosecutor. "I think, Mr. Prosecutor," he said, "that by the time you think over the entire evidence in this case, you will realize that you are proceeding against the wrong defendant, and that the very greatest favor the Court could do you at this time would be to dismiss the case against the defendant.

"You are here asking for an order that this defendant, George Ansley, be bound over for trial, and the Court feels that if such an order should be made, it would put you in a position where at a later date you would either have to dismiss the case against George Ansley, or, if you went to trial before a jury, you would have a verdict of acquittal at the hands of the jury.

"The Court realizes thoroughly that it is not incumbent upon the prosecution to put on all of its evidence in a preliminary examination, that in general the purpose of the examination is simply to show that a crime has been committed and that there is reasonable cause to believe the defendant has committed that crime. However, there is another duty which devolves upon the prosecutor, and that is to conduct his office in the interests of justice and to see that the innocent are released and not subjected to the annoyance and expense of trial, and that the guilty are prosecuted.

"The Court feels that, with the facts in this case brought into evidence as they now are, there is every indication that the defendant is being prosecuted for a crime that he did not commit, for a crime that he could not have committed.

"It is not incumbent on this Court to suggest to the prosecutor how the office of the district attorney should be conducted. But the Court does suggest that in this case further action should be taken and against an entirely different defendant.

"As far as this instant proceeding is concerned, the case against George Ansley is dismissed. The defendant is discharged from custody, and court is adjourned."

Judge Erwood arose and strode from the courtroom.

There was a demonstration among the spectators. Newspaper reporters dashed for the nearest telephones, and Mason turned to shake hands with George Ansley.

Photographers exploded flashbulbs as Hamilton Burger, glowering at the group around Mason, pushed his angry way through the spectators, strode out of the courtroom and down the corridor.

Chapter 13

It was well after nine-thirty in the morning when Mason unlocked the door of his private office, grinned at Della Street and said, "The newspapers didn't do very well by our friend Hamilton Burger."

Della Street laughed. "As a matter of good public relations, he should have at least hung around the courtroom and talked with some of the reporters. Pushing the reporters to one side and striding down the corridor didn't do him any good."

"So I see in the press," Mason said. "Well, here we are, starting all over again. What's new — anything?"

"You have another client," Della Street said.

"What kind of a case?" Mason asked.

"Murder."

"Indeed! Who's been murdered now?"

"Meridith Borden."

Mason raised his eyebrows.

"Dawn Manning telephoned," Della Street

said. "She is in *durance vile*. She said that she had been permitted to telephone for an attorney, and that she wanted you to represent her."

"Where is she?"

"Up in the women's section of Detention," Della Street said.

Mason walked over and picked up his hat. "You're going?"

"Sure, I'm going."

"Chief, can you take her case after — ?"

"After what?" Mason asked.

"After virtually accusing her of murder in court yesterday."

"Did I accuse her of murder?"

"You did — at least by innuendo. And so did Judge Erwood."

Mason said, "All the time I was discussing the matter, I was thinking what an embarrassing situation Hamilton Burger was going to find himself in if he charged Dawn Manning with the crime."

"What do you mean? There's virtually a perfect case against her. You can see what she did. She was thrown out of that car, she retained the gun, she found herself in the Borden grounds, she went to keep an appointment with Meridith Borden. The evidence is all there. She can't possibly deny her presence in view of the new testimony of the unde-

278

veloped photographs in the camera. She's got to admit that she was there with him, and once she admits that, she has to admit she's lied. . . . Oh, Chief, don't get mixed up in *her* case."

"Why not?"

"Well, for one thing," Della Street said, "suppose Hamilton Burger should manipulate things so that the preliminary hearing comes up in front of Judge Erwood. You know how Judge Erwood feels; his temper, his ideas about the administration of justice, and the way he feels about the duties of attorneys as officers of the court. He'd *really* be laying for you this time."

"It's a challenge," Mason said, "and Dawn Manning is a very beautiful woman."

Della Street said, "Chief, let me make a prediction. If the grapevine from the jail shows that you went up to see her, Hamilton Burger will manipulate things so that the preliminary hearing will come up before Judge Erwood. I'll bet you ten to one on it."

Mason thought that over and said, "No takers, Della. I think you're right. I think that's exactly what he'll do. It's what I would do if I were in Hamilton Burger's position."

"Well," Della Street said, "Judge Erwood will — He'll . . . he'll throw everything at you, including the kitchen sink."

"I'm good at dodging," Mason said. "If any-body wants me for the next hour, I'll be up talking with Dawn Manning, and I rather think we'll take her case, Della."

Chapter 14

Mason sat in the visitor's room and looked across through the thick, glass panel at Dawn Manning.

The heavy sheet of plate glass kept them separated, but a microphone on each side enabled them to hear each other.

She surveyed him with cool, slate-gray eyes and said, "Well, you certainly sold *me* down the river!"

"*I* did?" Mason asked.

"You don't need to apologize," she said. "When you represent a client, you go all out for that client. You were representing George Ansley then, and you could get him off by tossing me to the wolves. The question is, how good a job you and that wonderful husband of mine have done in framing me."

"Did you call me up here to berate me for what happened?" Mason asked.

"I did not. I want you to be my lawyer."

"Well?" Mason asked.

"And I haven't a lot to pay on a fee. But

I do feel that you owe me some consideration."

Mason said, "The fee won't be the most important thing. The most important thing is whether you told me the truth when you talked with me."

"I told you the truth. Well, anyway, most of it."

"You knew that Frank hadn't secured a divorce?"

"I had just found it out."

"You knew that Loretta was his girl friend?"

"I knew that he was playing around with a Loretta Harper, but I didn't know her from Eve. I didn't know her when I saw her."

"But you had modeled for Meridith Borden?"

"Of course. I told you about that. I had, however, never modeled for him in the nude, and I don't know where those pictures came from. I wasn't in the house that night. I didn't like Meridith Borden. He . . . well, I told you he wanted to use me as bait for some sort of a badger game, or to get the goods on some official. I don't go for that sort of thing. I walked out."

"Was there a scene?"

"There was one hell of a scene. I slapped his dirty face."

"Can the district attorney prove that?"

"Of course he can. Meridith Borden tried

to — Well, there was a scene."

"Others were present?"

"Yes."

"Did you threaten to kill him?"

"I said I'd shoot him like a dog. . . . Oh, I suppose I'm in one hell of a position!"

"*Did* you kill him?"

"No. I told you the truth. I walked out of the grounds as soon as I knew where I was."

"Then how did it happen he took your pictures in the nude?"

"He didn't."

"The camera says he did, and cameras don't lie."

"I can't explain those pictures, Mr. Mason, but I wasn't there."

"You do pose in the nude?"

"For photographers I know and for what are known as 'art' nudes, yes. I've posed thousands of times for calendar pictures, both in color and in black and white."

"Did you have a gun?" Mason asked.

"I *never* had a gun."

"Never carried one?"

"No, of course not."

Mason said, "You get into situations at times where you probably need some protection."

"What do you mean by that?"

"You're out with photographers in the

wilds, being photographed in skimpy bathing suits, and —"

"And you don't try to conceal a .38-caliber revolver in the folds of a bikini bathing suit, Mr. Mason," she interrupted. "A model learns to take care of herself. You do it one way or another, but you don't carry guns."

Mason said, "Okay, Dawn, I'm your attorney."

Chapter 15

Judge Erwood looked down at the jammed courtroom, said acidly, "The People of the State of California versus Dawn Ferney, also known as Dawn Manning. This is the time fixed for the preliminary hearing."

"We're ready, Your Honor," Hamilton Burger said.

Judge Erwood said, "Does the Court understand that Mr. Mason is representing this defendant?"

"That is quite right, Your Honor," Mason said.

Judge Erwood said, "The last time you were in this court, Mr. Mason, you were presenting evidence which pointed the finger of suspicion very strongly at this defendant."

"That evidence will now be presented by the district attorney," Mason said, smiling, "and I will be permitted to cross-examine the witnesses."

Judge Erwood hesitated a moment, as though casting about in his mind for some ground on which he could administer a rebuke, then he said, "Proceed, Mr. District Attorney."

Hamilton Burger delegated the preliminaries to his associate counsel, Sam Drew, who once more introduced evidence as to the location of the premises, the finding of the body, the location and identification of the fatal bullet, the firing of test bullets through the gun which had been recovered from Ansley's car, and the identification of the fatal bullet with the test bullet. Now the pictures of Dawn Manning which had been found in Borden's studio were introduced by the prosecution as a telling point in its case.

"My next witness will be Harvey Dennison," Hamilton Burger said.

Harvey Dennison came forward, was sworn and once again told the story of the missing gun.

"Any cross-examination?" Judge Erwood asked Mason.

"Yes, Your Honor."

Mason arose and stood by the edge of the counsel table, looking at Harvey Dennison with steady eyes. "Mr. Dennison, I take it you have consulted the records of the store in order to get the information on which your testimony is based?"

"Yes, sir."

"The defendant was working for you during the period when the gun was found to be missing?"

"Yes, sir."

"You can't tell the date when the gun was taken?"

"No, sir."

"As I understand your testimony, your records show that the gun was ordered and received from the wholesaler on a certain date, that, at a later date, perhaps some months later, you took an inventory and found that the gun was not in your stock."

"That's right."

"How many employees did you have in your store?"

"You mean as salesclerks?"

"No, I mean your total employees."

"Well, counting bookkeepers, stock clerks, salespersons, we've had — let me see, about twelve, I think."

"Including the owners?"

"No, sir."

"How many owners are there?"

"Three."

"So there was a total of fifteen persons who could have taken that gun?"

"Well . . . yes, sir, I guess so."

"And, during the time between the date the gun was received by you and the date when it was found to be missing when an inventory was taken, there were two burglaries of the store, were there not?"

"Yes, sir,"

"And what was taken in those burglaries?"

"Objected to as incompetent, irrelevant and immaterial, and not proper cross-examination," Burger snapped.

Judge Erwood said, "I think you should limit your question somewhat, Mr. Mason."

"Very well, I will. I'll withdraw that question and ask Mr. Dennison if it isn't true that sporting goods were taken when the store was burglarized on each occasion."

"Same objection," Hamilton Burger said.

"Overruled," Judge Erwood snapped.

"Yes, sir," Dennison admitted. "As nearly as we could tell, all that was taken on those occasions was hunting and fishing material, and some cash."

"What do you mean by hunting and fishing material?"

"Ammunition, rifles, shotguns, fishing rods, reels."

"On both occasions the material taken consisted solely of sporting goods?"

"And money."

"Both times?"

"Yes."

"No further questions," Mason said.

"Just a moment," Hamilton Burger said. "I have one or two on redirect. If that gun had been taken on the occasion of either of those burglaries, you would have found that it was missing at that time, isn't that correct?"

"Objected to as argumentative, leading and suggestive, and calling for a conclusion of the witness," Mason said.

"Sustained," Judge Erwood said.

"Well, you took an inventory after each of those burglaries, didn't you?"

"Yes, sir."

"Now then, I am going to ask you if you found that this gun was missing immediately after either one of the burglaries?"

"No, sir."

"That's all," Hamilton Burger said.

Mason smiled.

"Did either of those inventories disclose this gun as being present?"

"No, sir, it did not. As I have said, something happened to our records on this gun. I don't understand it exactly, but all I can state is that the gun was *not* sold over the counter."

"That's all," Mason said, smiling.

"And during the time of this shortage, the defendant was in your employ?" Hamilton Burger asked.

"That's right."

"No further questions," Hamilton Burger said.

"And fourteen other people were also in your employ?" Mason asked.

"Well, yes."

"No further questions," Mason said.

"That's all," Hamilton Burger announced. "Mr. Dennison will be excused. I will now call Frank Ferney. I may state to the Court that in some respects Mr. Ferney is an unwilling witness. He has, I believe, tried to protect this defendant wherever possible, and —"

Mason arose.

Hamilton Burger said, "And I may have to ask leading questions in order to get at the truth. I think this witness has perhaps —"

"Just a moment," Judge Erwood said. "Do you wish to object, Mr. Mason?"

"Yes, Your Honor, I feel that it is incumbent on the district attorney to ask questions, and then, if it appears the witness is hostile, he can ask leading questions. But I see no reason for the prosecution to make a speech at this time, a speech which is quite evidently intended to arouse sympathy for this witness."

"The Court feels Mr. Mason is correct, Mr. Burger. Just go ahead and ask your questions."

"Very well," Hamilton Burger said. "Your

name is Frank Ferney?"

"That is right."

"You were employed by Meridith Borden at the time of his death?"

"That's right."

"Now, directing your attention to the night when Mr. Borden was murdered, the night of the eighth, were you at Meridith Borden's house on that night?"

"Yes, sir."

"At about what time?"

"Just a moment," Mason said, "if the Court please, at this point I wish to object to this question and ask that this witness be instructed not to answer any questions as to anything that happened on the night of the eighth."

Judge Erwood showed surprise. "On what grounds?" he asked.

"On the ground that the witness is married to the defendant, that the relationship of husband and wife exists, and that a husband cannot be examined for or against his wife without the consent of the wife."

"Just a minute," Hamilton Burger said, "I'll clear that up. *Are* you married to the defendant, Mr. Ferney?"

"No, sir."

"You are *not* her husband?"

"No, sir."

Hamilton Burger grinned at Perry Mason.

"May I ask a question on that, Your Honor?" Mason asked.

"Very well, on that particular point only," Judge Erwood said.

"You married the defendant at one time?"

"Yes, sir."

"When?"

"Some three years ago."

"You have been living separate and apart for some period of time?"

"Yes, sir."

"How long?"

"About eighteen months."

"And you have now divorced this defendant?"

"Yes, sir."

"When was that divorce decree granted?"

"Yesterday."

"Where?"

"In Reno, Nevada."

"I take it you flew to Reno, Nevada, obtained your decree and flew back here in order to be a witness?"

"Yes, sir."

"You had previously filed this suit for divorce, the issues had been joined, but you hadn't gone through with the divorce?"

"That's right."

"You *were* married to the defendant on

the night of the eighth when the murder was committed?"

"Yes, sir."

"That's all, Your Honor," Mason said.

"But you aren't married to her *now*," Hamilton Burger said. "There is no longer any relationship of husband and wife."

"That's right," Ferney said.

"If the Court please," Hamilton Burger said, "I am prepared to argue this point. People versus Godines 17 Cal App 2nd 721, and the case of People versus Loper 159 California 6 112 Pacific 720, both hold that a divorced spouse is not prohibited from testifying even to anything that happened during the period the marriage was in force."

Mason said, "Doesn't the case of People versus Mullings 83 California 138 23 Pacific 229, and Kansas City Life Insurance Company versus Jones 21 Fed Sup 159 hold that a divorced wife cannot testify as to confidential communications between herself and the accused while they were married?"

"Who's asking about any confidential communications?" Hamilton Burger shouted. "I'm asking about facts."

"Aren't you going to ask him if he didn't knock on the door of Borden's studio and hear his wife's voice say, 'Go away'?" Mason inquired.

"Certainly," Burger snapped.

"There you are," Mason said. "That's a privileged communication between husband and wife. This witness can't testify to that, both under the provisions of Subdivision 1 of Section 1881 of our Code of Civil Procedure, as well as Section 1332 of the Penal Code."

Hamilton Burger's eyes widened in astonishment. "That's not what the law had in mind in regard to privileged communications between husband and wife. The defendant merely spoke to this witness without knowing she was addressing her husband."

"How do you know what she knew?" Mason asked.

Burger, so angry he was all but sputtering, said, "Your Honor, if the Court should enforce any such rule, it would mean that the defendant in this case would be allowed to get by with murder. And I mean literally to get by with murder. She has committed the crime of murder. A witness is now on the stand who knows facts that force us to the conclusion that this defendant committed the crime. They are no longer husband and wife, they have been living separate and apart for over a year, there is no relationship between them which the law should encourage. The reason for the rule has ceased, and so the rule itself should cease."

"Whatever a wife may have said to her husband is a confidential and therefore a privileged communication," Mason said. "If this defendant was in that room and asked her husband to go away, she was appealing to him as his spouse. She was his wife at that time."

"Poppycock!" Hamilton Burger exploded. "She had no idea who it was at the door. She only knew someone had knocked and she didn't want the door opened while she was standing there in the nude."

"Not at all," Mason said. "If the witness could have recognized his wife's voice, she could have recognized his."

"But she didn't mean it as a *confidential* communication," Burger said.

Mason smiled. "If you're going to testify as to what my client *thought*, Mr. District Attorney, you'll have to get on the stand, and then you'll have to qualify as a mind reader. You'll probably need your crystal ball to hold in your hands while you're testifying."

Judge Erwood, fighting back a smile, said, "Let's not have any more personalities, gentlemen. In the face of the objection on the part of the defense, Mr. District Attorney, this Court is going to sustain the objection to anything it is claimed a wife said to her husband while the marriage was in existence, particularly at a time when she was in a room where a corpse was subsequently found."

"But, if the Court please," Hamilton Burger protested, "that simply tears the middle right out of our case. We don't have a leg to stand on unless we can rely on the testimony of this witness."

"Just a moment," Judge Erwood said. "Let me point out to you, Mr. District Attorney, that in this court you are not building up a case to prove the defendant guilty beyond all reasonable doubt. You only need to establish a *prima facie* case. That is, that the murder has been committed (a fact which you have now established), and that there is reasonable ground to believe the defendant committed that crime. You have proven she had an opportunity to possess herself of the murder weapon. Now, all you need to do is to prove the presence of the defendant on the premises at the time the crime could have been committed. That's all you need to establish in *this* court.

"You can then take this question of evidence to the superior court, where it can be properly ruled upon and after the ruling can be properly reviewed."

Hamilton Burger thought that over.

"I take it," Mason said, "that the Court is not intimating in advance what its decision will be."

Judge Erwood frowned down at Mason. "The Court is not precluding the defense from putting on any evidence it may desire, if that is what you mean. If this evidence indicates that the defendant should be released, the defendant will be released.

"However, the Court *is* stating that if the evidence in this case, when it is all in, tends to prove that this defendant probably had possession of the weapon with which the murder was committed, at the time of the murder, that the murder was committed at a time *when* the defendant was on the grounds *where* the murder was committed, the Court will consider that as sufficient evidence to make an order binding the defendant over."

"Very well," Hamilton Burger said, his face brightening somewhat. "We'll withdraw you from the stand, Mr. Ferney, and call Loretta Harper."

Loretta Harper was sworn and testified that she had been giving a party in her apartment, that Jason and Millicent Kendell, two very old friends, were there in the apartment, that she had left shortly before nine o'clock to run across the street and get some cigarettes, that a Cadillac had slowed down opposite her while she was in the crosswalk, that the defendant had been in the car, that the defendant had accused her of "playing around" with the defendant's husband and keeping the defendant's husband from getting a divorce.

The defendant had ordered Loretta into the automobile with her at the point of a gun.

Loretta went on to testify about being taken out to Meridith Borden's place along the wet roads, about the defendant driving with one hand, about the car skidding and overturning. She admitted that she substituted herself for the defendant in order to try to keep her name from getting in the papers, that she had then told George Ansley that her name was Beatrice Cornell in order to keep herself from becoming "involved," and had had him drive her to the Ancordia Apartments, from which she had taken a taxicab back to her own apartment where she had suddenly realized her fiancé, Frank Ferney, had failed to keep an appointment with Dr. Callison and had aroused him from a deep sleep and started him hurrying to Dr. Callison's veterinary hospital.

"You may cross-examine," Hamilton Burger said.

"You occupy an apartment in the Dormain Apartments?" Mason asked.

"Yes."

"What is the number of that apartment?"

"409."

"It is your recollection that the defendant was holding a gun in her hand at the time of the accident?"

"Yes."

"Did you see that gun after the accident?"

"I did not."

"Did you look at her hands after the accident to see whether she was still holding the gun?"

"I did not, but I don't think the gun was in her hands. I think it had been thrown out somewhere and was doubtless lying on the grass."

"No further questions," Mason said.

Hamilton Burger thought for a moment, then said, "If the Court please, that's our case."

"Well," Judge Erwood said, "it's not a particularly robust case, but the Court can well understand that it is only a technicality which keeps it from being a *very* robust case. This is, of course, the second time the facts in this case have been called to the Court's attention. Does the defense wish to make any showing, Mr. Mason?"

"It does, Your Honor."

"Very well, put on whatever evidence you have," Judge Erwood said in a tone which plainly indicated that evidence would do no good.

"My first witness is Beatrice Cornell," Mason said.

Beatrice Cornell took the stand, testified to her name, address and occupation.

"Was the defendant, Dawn Manning, listed with you as one of the models you had available to be sent out on photographic work?"

"She was."

"And that was on the eighth of this month?"

"Yes."

"On the ninth of this month did someone ask you to have Dawn Manning go out on a job?"

"Yes."

"And did you have occasion to see Dawn Manning's body, particularly the area around her left hip, on that date?"

"I did."

"Can you describe the condition of that hip?"

"From the hipbone down along the thigh, she was scraped. Part of the scraping was simply a mild scrape which had left a bruise and a discoloration, but there were two or three places where the skin had been taken completely away."

"Leaving unsightly bruises?" Mason asked.

"Yes."

"Do you know whether she was photographed on the morning of the ninth?"

"She was."

"I show you a color photograph and ask you what that picture is."

"It is a picture showing Dawn Manning,

taken on the ninth. It shows the condition of her left thigh and the left hip."

"Cross-examine," Mason said to Hamilton Burger.

The district attorney smiled. "In other words, Miss Cornell, everything that you have noticed substantiates the story told by the prosecution's witness, Loretta Harper, that the defendant had been in an accident the night before?"

"Yes."

"Thank you," Hamilton Burger said, bowing and smiling. "That's all." And then he couldn't resist turning to Mason and bowing and smiling and saying, "And thank *you*, Mr. Mason."

"Not at all," Mason told him. "My next witness will be Morley Edmond."

Morley Edmond was called to the stand, qualified himself as an expert photographer, a member of several photographic societies, a veteran of several salon exhibitions, winner of numerous photographic awards, contributor to various photographic magazines.

"I now show you certain pictures of the defendant which have heretofore been introduced in evidence, and ask you if you are familiar with those pictures."

"I am."

"You've seen them before?"

"I've studied them carefully."

"I will ask you if you are familiar with the studio camera which was in the photographic studio of Meridith Borden."

"I am."

"Can you tell us whether or not these pictures were taken with that camera?"

"I can."

"Were they?"

"Just a minute, just a minute," Hamilton Burger said. "Don't answer that question until I have an opportunity to interpose an objection. Your Honor, this is something I have never encountered before in all of my experience. This question calls for an opinion and a conclusion of a witness in a matter where the physical evidence speaks for itself. Of course the pictures were taken with that camera. They were found in the camera."

"What is your specific objection?" Judge Erwood asked.

"That the question calls for the opinion of the witness, that no proper foundation has been laid, and that it is in a case where the issue on which this witness is expected to testify cannot be covered by expert testimony."

Judge Erwood looked at Perry Mason.

Mason merely smiled and said, "We propose to *prove* to the Court that the pictures of the defendant were planted in that camera, that they couldn't have been taken with that camera."

"But how in the world can you prove whether a picture was taken with a certain camera?" Judge Erwood asked.

"That," Mason said, "is what I am trying to illustrate to the Court."

"I'll permit the question," Judge Erwood said, leaning forward curiously. "However, the Court would want to have some very, very good reasons from this expert, otherwise a motion to strike the testimony would be entertained."

"We'll give the Court reasons," Mason said. "Just answer the question, Mr. Edmond. Were those pictures, in your opinion, taken with the Meridith Borden camera?"

"They were not."

"And on what reasons do you base your opinion?"

"The size of the image."

"Explain what you mean by that."

"The size of the image on a photographic plate," Edmond said, "is determined by the focal length of the lens and the distance of the subject from the camera.

"If the lens has a very short focal length, with reference to the area that is to be covered, the lens usually gives a wider field of coverage on the photographic plate, but the size of the object is smaller. If the focal length of the lens is very large, with reference to the area of the plate, the image shown is shown in larger size but with a very small field.

"In order to get a proper plate coverage, it is generally conceded that the standard focal length of the lens should be the diagonal of the plate to be covered. However, in portrait work it is generally considered that a focal-length lens of one and a half or two times the diagonal will result in more pleasing proportions.

"A rather simple illustration of what I mean has doubtless been noticed by Your Honor in television photography. When the television camera is focused, for instance, on the second baseman, a long focal-length lens is used in order to build up the image. At that time, if the Court has perhaps noticed, the center fielder seems to be within only a few feet of the second baseman. In other words, the perspective is distorted so that it no longer bears the ordinary relationship which the eye has accepted as standard in photographic reproductions.

"To some extent, this principle makes for a better portrait of a face, and, therefore, the longer focal-length lens is used in portrait photography."

"But what does all this have to do with

whether the picture of the defendant was taken with Meridith Borden's camera?" Judge Erwood asked.

"Simply this, Your Honor: The full-length picture of the defendant shown on the photographic films occupies but little more than one-half of the perpendicular distance. With the longer focal-length lens used by Meridith Borden in his camera, and taking into consideration the dimensions of his studio, it is a physical impossibility to take a full-length which will occupy only one-half of the perpendicular distance of the film. Even if the camera is placed at one corner of the studio and the model at the other corner so that we have the maximum distance permitted within the room, the image on a five-by-seven plate or cut film would be materially larger than that shown on the developed plates.

"Therefore, I have been forced to the inescapable conclusion that these pictures of the defendant were taken with some other camera and then, before those pictures were developed, the film holders were placed in the Meridith Borden studio, and one of the film holders bearing an exposed film was placed inside the camera itself.

"However, for the physical reasons stated, none of these pictures could have been taken with the Borden camera."

"Cross-examine," Mason said.

Hamilton Burger's voice was sharp with sarcasm. "You think because you found a certain focal-length lens in the Borden camera, the photographs of the defendant couldn't have been taken with that camera and that lens."

"I know that they couldn't have been."

"Despite the fact that all the physical evidence shows that they must have been taken with that camera?"

"That is right."

"In other words, you're like the man who went to the zoo, saw a giraffe and said, 'There isn't any such animal.' "

There was laughter in the courtroom.

"That question is facetious, Mr. District Attorney," Judge Erwood said.

"I think not, Your Honor. I think it is perfectly permissible."

"I have made no objection," Mason said.

"I'm not like that man at all," the witness said. "I know photography and I know what can be done and what can't be done. I have made test exposures using a duplicate of the Borden camera, and at various distances. I used a model having exactly the same measurements as the defendant as far as height is concerned. Those pictures were taken on five-by-seven films with a lens that had the same focal length as that in the Borden camera.

I have compared the image sizes. I can produce those films, if necessary."

"No further questions," Hamilton Burger said. "*I'm* going to rely on the physical evidence in this case, and I think His Honor will also."

"Call James Goodwin to the stand," Mason said.

James Goodwin testified that he was an architect, that he had designed the apartment house known as the Dormain Apartments, that he had his various plans showing the apartment house, and he identified and introduced in evidence a floor plan of the fourth floor.

Hamilton Burger gave a contemptuous glance at the floor plan and said, "No questions," when Mason turned the witness over for cross-examination.

"That's all of our evidence, Your Honor," Mason said.

"Do you have any rebuttal?" Judge Erwood asked Hamilton Burger.

"None, Your Honor. It certainly appears that there is reasonable ground to believe the defendant committed the crime. The testimony of Loretta Harper standing alone is sufficient to warrant an order binding the defendant over."

"May I be heard in argument?" Mason asked.

"I don't think it is necessary, Mr. Mason, nor do I think it would do any good. However, I'll not preclude you from arguing the case."

"Thank you, Your Honor."

"The prosecution has the right to open the argument," Judge Erwood said.

Hamilton Burger, smiling, said, "We waive our opening argument."

"Proceed, Mr. Mason," Judge Erwood said.

"If the Court please," Mason said, "I claim that this case is a frame-up. Those pictures of the defendant were not taken in Meridith Borden's photographic studio. We have the evidence of the camera expert, that the photographs could not have been taken with Meridith Borden's camera. And now, if the Court please, I will call the Court's attention to one other item of physical evidence. The Court will note that according to the testimony of Loretta Harper, the defendant had been thrown from the car and had skidded along on her hip. Thereafter, the witness had dragged the defendant a still further distance on her hip.

"The Court will notice that the next day the hip of the defendant was so bruised and scraped that she could not pose as a model for any so-called cheesecake shots.

"Now then, if the Court will carefully examine the photographs which purport to have been taken with the camera in Meridith Borden's studio at a time *after* the accident, the Court will find irrefutable evidence that these pictures were taken at some time prior to the night of the murder and then planted in the Borden camera.

"Bear in mind that this defendant is a professional model. She poses almost daily for amateur photographers who are interested in various types of photography, particularly the so-called cheesecake pictures.

"It would have been readily possible for any accomplice to have paid this defendant her posing rate, have taken these pictures and then have held them for as long a period of time as desired until finally turning them over to the murderer of Meridith Borden to be planted in the camera of the victim.

"If the Court will carefully study the left hip of the defendant, as shown in the Borden photographs, the Court will see that there are absolutely no grass stains, no mud-stains, no scrapes, no blemishes of any sort. It would have been a physical impossibility for the defendant to have been photographed immediately after that accident without some of these defects showing.

"For the benefit of the Court, I wish to call the Court's attention to this picture of the defendant which was taken the day after the accident, and which shows the extent of the scrapes and bruises on the defendant's left hip.

"The Court will notice that the defendant worked at the Valley View Hardware Company until her marriage. In other words, it is reasonable to suppose that Frank Ferney was courting her during the time she was engaged as a clerk in that store.

"Someone stole the murder weapon from the store. That thief was a man. If the defendant had been dishonest enough to steal a weapon for her own protection, she would have taken one of the small automatics of a type that could be placed in her purse. This weapon is a man's weapon. It was stolen by a man. It is reasonable to suppose that Frank Ferney was in and out of the store many times, and, enjoying the confidence of the defendant, that he was permitted behind the counter.

"Turning to the so-called time schedule, or alibi of Frank Ferney, I ask the Court to notice the plans which have been introduced by James Goodwin showing the fourth floor of the apartment house where Loretta Harper has her apartment.

"It is to be remembered that Frank Ferney was supposed to have passed out and to have been placed in this bedroom to sleep it off. The Court will notice that the fire escape runs right past this bedroom in 409. It was a simple matter for Ferney to slip out of the window, go down the fire escape, go to Meridith Borden's house, commit the murder and return in time to be aroused from his apparent sleep when Loretta Harper came in to tell the spectacular story of her kidnaping.

"I think it is a fair inference that there was a deliberate attempt on the part of Loretta Harper and Frank Ferney to kill Meridith Borden and to do it under such circumstances that the crime would be blamed on this defendant.

"The evidence of that frame-up not only exists in the extrinsic evidence in this case, but, if the Court will carefully study the pictures which were taken of this defendant, and which were in Meridith Borden's camera, the Court will realize that those pictures simply couldn't have been taken on the night of the murder."

Mason sat down.

Judge Erwood frowned, said, "Let me look at those pictures."

He started comparing the Borden pictures with the photograph Mason had taken of the hip of Dawn Manning.

Hamilton Burger jumped to his feet. "That's all very simple, Your Honor. Just a little retouching would have fixed up those pictures."

"But these pictures haven't been retouched," Judge Erwood said. "The films are here in Court."

Hamilton Burger slowly sat down.

Abruptly Judge Erwood reached his decision. "I think some more investigative work needs to be done in this case," he said. "I am going to dismiss the case and discharge the defendant from custody. The Court is satisfied there is something peculiar here, and the Court feels that there should be a much more careful check of the evidence.

"The defendant is discharged, the case is dismissed, and court is adjourned."

Chapter 16

Perry Mason, Della Street, Paul Drake, George Ansley and Dawn Manning sat in the lawyer's private office.

"Well," Dawn Manning said, "I have to hand it to you, Mr. Mason. I certainly thought you had tossed me to the wolves."

"I did," Mason admitted, "but then I came along with another car and picked you up before the wolves got there."

"Just what do you think happened?" Della Street asked.

Mason said, "I think that Meridith Borden had caught Frank Ferney in some theft or embezzlement. I believe Borden handled large sums of money in the form of cash which were passed out here and there as bribes and which were received by various people. Borden didn't dare to have checks made so they could be traced on his bank account. He didn't give checks.

"It is reasonable to suppose that with that much cash around, Frank Ferney had managed to embezzle some. The probabilities are he was about to be discovered, or perhaps he had been discovered and Borden had decided to report the case to the police.

"An elaborate plan was worked out by which Dawn Manning would have been brought on the grounds immediately after nine o'clock and then left there. She would have been escorted to the photographic studio by Loretta Harper. In the meantime, Frank Ferney would apparently have been nowhere around. Loretta Harper, who was driving a stolen car so that the car and the driver couldn't be traced from the license plates, would have asked Dawn to excuse her for a moment, telling Dawn to go ahead and run up to the studio. Then Loretta would have vanished. She would have been back at her apartment in time to corroborate Frank Ferney's alibi.

"However, everything depended upon split-second timing. It was necessary to kill Meridith Borden precisely at a certain minute, so that Ferney could get back at the apartment house, climb up the fire escape and get into bed. The understanding was that he was to be aroused in order to keep his appointment with Dr. Callison.

"Ferney carried out his end of the bargain right on schedule. George Ansley's visit had been unexpected. As soon as Ansley left and Borden had telephoned the inspectors, Ferney lured Meridith Borden up into the studio and killed him. Then he waited impatiently for the arrival of the car with Dawn Manning.

"For reasons that we know, that car didn't arrive.

"That called on Ferney to do some quick thinking. For one thing, he decided he'd have to change the time of the murder to a time when Loretta Harper would also have an alibi. Dr. Callison was going to be his alibi.

"It wasn't until the next day, after it was seen how far their original plan had gone awry, that it was decided to plant the murder gun in the glove compartment of George Ansley's automobile and blame the murder on him. For a while they thought they could get away with it. Then, when it appeared that I was knocking holes in their case against Ansley, Loretta Harper, who was the shrewder of the pair, signaled Frank Ferney to go back to their original plan and blame the crime on Dawn Manning."

The telephone rang.

Della Street picked up the receiver, said, "It's for you, Paul."

Drake took the phone, listened for several moments, then said, "Thanks, let me know if there are any more details." He hung up and turned to Mason.

"Well," he said, "your hunch was right. Ferney has just broken down and confessed. The details are just about the way you figured them. Ferney knew that he was trapped, so now he's trying to blame Loretta as the originator of the scheme. The D.A. found a witness who saw a man going down the fire escape from the fourth floor of the Dormain Apartments. If the police had been on the job, they'd have had the information long ago, because the witness telephoned in to the police station to report a prowler. The Mesa Vista police went out, looked the place over and then did nothing more about it."

"Well," Dawn Manning said, "I've heard of people getting out of trouble by the skin of their eyeteeth. I never thought it would apply to me."

There was a twinkle in Della Street's eye. "Not your eyeteeth," she said demurely.

The employees of THORNDIKE PRESS hope you have enjoyed this Large Print book. All our Large Print titles are designed for easy reading, and all our books are made to last. Other Thorndike Large Print books are available at your library, through selected bookstores, or directly from us. For more information about current and upcoming titles, please call or mail your name and address to:

THORNDIKE PRESS
PO Box 159
Thorndike, Maine 04986
800/223-6121
207/948-2962